TITLE PA(

CW01638537

Denis McClean

ISBN 978-0-9926814-8-7 Second Edition

Thank you for respecting the work that goes into my books, which is the only way I can create more of them by return.

For updates on my published and latest work, please visit me at my Blog, which will point you to my Web-Site and also to my Facebook Page.

http://denismcclean.blogspot.ie/

Skellig is the fourth and last of the current '**Thin Places**' Series of Novellas after **Fanore, Erris and Blasket**. At this time of publication, **Fanore** is still a free download but only from my web-site and from my blog. It should not be available from any other source. You therefore have the option to get one for nothing, two for the price of one, three for two or four for three.

Because every story should be told in its entirety, Skellig took longer to write than anticipated and it's also too big to be a novella as such. But then, what is Skellig if not an opportunity to bend silly notions into shape.

Enjoy.

DEDICATION

To:- Cathal McClean

Master and Commander, he is.

ACKNOWLEDGEMENTS

This is the fourth and maybe the last of my 'Thin Places' series of novellas for now, even though technically, this one is too big to be a novella. Some stories steadfastly refuse to be cropped and that has to be good news for readers. I made sincere efforts to log all sources of hard fact, superstition and inspiration that went into creating the journey you are about to undertake but there were many. So I apologise profusely for any omissions.

First and foremost, thanks to Gina and Grainne for their steadfast application to proof-reading and general critique. One is a stickler for grammar, while the other is a huge fan of virtual escape through writing, which also makes them quality assurance.

Phil McClean (The Real Phil McClean) co-inspired the concept some time ago. His music has seriously evolved but in an early composition he told the story of a heretic priest drawn into a wasteland to confront his demons. Skellig is a vastly different proposition, and even though my priest is not possessed by demons per se, the concept also struck a chord with me back then. There is something very compelling about someone who unconditionally dedicates absolutely everything, only to be forced by circumstance to re-evaluate their motives. I also discovered that Jesuits are nothing if not specialists at introspection.

Grateful thanks to Howard Goldbaum for the unbelievable depth, quality and quantity of material made freely available through his portal, (Voices from the dawn). This is a man who's been getting his fingers and boots dirty for 40 years in a bewildering array of ancient Irish archeological sites and then presenting their uniqueness for our armchair appreciation. I followed his extensive map to Skellig for insights into Bronze Age and early Christian Life in Ireland.

Catholicireland.net and the Diocese of Kerry at http://www.dioceseofkerry.ie/our-diocese/genealogy/skellig/ both supplied remarkable detail into Ireland at the time of Saint Patrick. And because my priest is a Jesuit, I took advantage of Ignatianspirituality.com to get into the mindset of his 'official' version of Christianity. To ensure I didn't suffer tunnel vision, I was compelled to also visit Biblebelievers.org.au to see the less official dispensationalist viewpoint for reasons that will become apparent later. I also consulted Zaidpub.com to get the often critical Islamist perspective of the Christian Organisation. I haven't provided any links to overtly religious sites because this book doesn't promote any particular religious agenda.

Wikipedia proved once again that insight into virtually anything is always just a click away. It was particularly useful in getting some background into the countless heresies that were violently suppressed by church and states combined in the early years of the Roman Catholic Church.

It also proved to be a good place to start researching Zoroastrianism, Zen Buddhism and Celiac disorders alike.

Because it is a world heritage site, the Irish Government also plays its part in making archeological and historical research available and they do this quite well at: http://www.worldheritageireland.ie/skellig-michael/

Finally, like the other 3 books of this series, Fanore, Erris and Blasket, this one was supposed to be a mixture of fact, fiction and fantasy, but it's impossible to describe Skellig and totally disregard the spirituality that prevails. That also made it difficult to settle on any particular genre.

You might wonder why, if the book was not intended to be factual, that any actual research was necessary. The thing is, when so much of the entire setting is either fact or as close as makes no difference, and with so many of the characters taken from history, very little remains to be manufactured. This makes it easier to blur the lines between what was, what is and what can't be to make the most of your time-out.

THIN PLACES

You may not be entirely alone just now, but you are happy to be alone with your thoughts. In the mayhem of a world-on-steroids, that's probably as alone as you're likely to be for a while. So, 'Carpe Diem'.

We all need a little time to ourselves, but it's such a hard earned commodity these days. What I mean is, we too often waste it in idle self indulgence at the bottom of those rabbit holes we call our 'Private Headspaces? That's not to say that switching off to abstractly contemplate life from the usually callous perspectives of random third parties, doesn't have its merits. It's just that sometimes we've actually earned a more substantial break and we should take it, if for no other reason than to disrupt that cycle of give with more give and no take. Occasionally, we need to be taken much further from our cares and by opening these pages, you've invited me to take you somewhere really special. So, get comfortable and I don't mind waiting a few moments if you want to get that hot drink.

Now, I don't know what day it is where you are right now, but I hope it's warmer than it was at 3:57pm on a chilly Tuesday, when I won the argument with myself on how best to begin this introduction. The fact that you seem to be well-read tells me that you already know about 'Ice-Breakers' and I'm not talking about the guys who sail under the Auroras.

I'm referring to tools used by Human Resources, Recruitment and Training to help strangers like us get to know each other faster, so I thought it might be appropriate to use one here. And by the way, I'm not normally this pushy. It's just that even with your head stuck in a book, time still equals money, so let's get going.

Consider me the instructor setting the scene and regardless of whether you are proud or ashamed of the fact, you are a fully paid up and card-carrying member of Homo sapiens sapiens, so congrats on that but don't get carried away. You see, despite an evolution measured in billions years, people still perceive reality in only 3 or at most 4 dimensions, which is the same for a sightless worm. Thankfully, our brains work better than our eyes and we have theories to support 6, 7 or even 22 further space-time dimensions. The actual number will depend on which particular theory enjoys the blessing of your endorsement.

'They' suggest that the final dimension, whatever number we apply, is likely to be one in which all possibilities simultaneously exist and that has to make it infinite. Personally, I doubt that all possibilities can still exist because we do seem to excel in screwing up at least one tomorrow with every decision we make but then, how much smaller than infinity is infinity minus 1, 2 or even 3?

So, my 'Ice-Breaker' question is quite simple and it's this:

“Can you imagine what all of reality might really look like?”

I hear you mutter ‘sounds like work’ and I fully agree. I mean, that’s what you just paid me for, so I’ll just wait while you clamber over the central console there and flop into the passenger seat. And yes, I do see the keys dangling from the ignition. I don’t need to adjust the mirror, but I’m pretending to do it because I want you to see that I’m a good driver. That way, you can relax faster and not just because you fully deserve it, but because you’ll need to visualise all of ‘Reality’ to appreciate the ‘Thin Places’ aspect and they are both just a tad off the beaten track.

See? I do drive better than you and you know it, but you say nothing. The bonus for you is that you don’t have to tinker with your imaginary passenger-seat brake pedal and you're feeling just fine as you ease your seat back a notch or two, but hey … no sleeping OK? Our first problem is the fact that you can’t hope to see a reality composed of anywhere between 7 and 22 dimensions with eyes limited to just 3.

We might be practically blind but we are clever and so, we reason quite logically that infinity can only be seen from the last dimension, and the only way we can get there is by bringing our human imaginations into play. We compensate for our puny 3D perception by using our limitless imagination to visualise endless possibilities, and that brings us directly into the mysterious ultimate dimension.

There is just one more snag however, and that is the inconvenient fact that we can't really imagine something that we've never seen before, so we need to create that overview of reality with a logical analogy. Who needs eyes? So this is where you let me talk you through the analogy of the 'rope of reality' until you begin to 'see' everything, and I mean 'everything' for yourself.

We'll start by accepting the logic that everything that ever was or ever will be, must exist in either the past or the future. However, neither are as important as this present moment which is actually infinitesimal by comparison, but this instant is the 'perceived' total reality in which everything really exists. We consider everything else to be either conjecture or history.

So let's try to visualise the present reality as the sparking and hissing detonation cord that would normally be attached to a piece of dynamite in a cartoon, except there is no dynamite. Our cord is endless and it just burns through and then moves on as time passes, but it lies at the centre of a very substantial old rope, and all old ropes have sections that are worn or frayed. Time can do that.

Think of that heavy rope you once saw holding a ship to the quay and then think bigger ship and even bigger rope and you've got the right idea. Now, wound around that central detonating cord, you should also imagine the individual strands that make up our rope. They are usually coiled into a series of minor ropes which are then braided to make up the bigger rope to give it more strength. You probably noticed how some of those individual strands and fibres come with small kinks in them because nothing is perfect. I knew you'd be good at this.

Each of those fibres represents a future possibility, which is why our rope is big enough to contain every single one of them. Each of the countless strands represents a possibly impending event but here's the catch, only the strand that touches the central detonating cord as it burns and then passes further along the rope, will actually happen. That's because the future must interact with today to become fact and then pass into yesterday as dust, impossible to resurrect.

Some days are so action packed that we just can't keep up with them and others never seem to end, which is why the detonating cord sputters and sometimes looks like it's gone dead. But like any old flame, it can look dead and then suddenly come alive or jump ahead to stagnate again, maybe. We can't see that from outside the rope because it's all happening inside the fibres where we are, but it's happening nonetheless.

Past and future depend on the spark of today for their separate existences. So the first thing to appreciate is just how easy it is for the sputtering cord to go out for an instant, or to burn or scorch more than one fibre, or even ten. These will then coil away from the cord to light others which creates unpredictable parallel realities in which unscheduled, unlikely and even impossible events take place. Time seems to flow reasonably well where the central cord burns at the centre of the rope of time, but there's chaos when things occur without prelude or repercussion, where time just stops to restart somewhere or rather sometime in random fashion.

We're almost there and if you really did as I asked, you've also unconsciously imagined the beginning or the end of the rope, which is great because every rope is finite just like time itself. So, to complete our creation of an overview of everything, consider that the rope must rest in or on something, despite the fact that nothing can exist outside of everything. With that in mind, we can safely deduce no solid contact with the outer layers of rope, which can be directly exposed to infinity where they are frayed.

So, our rope snakes out weightlessly further and further into infinity as time burns through the centre. There is no structure and therefore no gravity beyond everything and time has a fixed length, so the rope never grows or shrinks. Today could be about to burn through the end of the rope but we won't know until we actually see infinity beyond for ourselves.

If you want to see it more detail, consider each individual strand to be thin, like fibreglass strands or optical fibres. These can be illuminated from the inside and colour coded for the past, which might be grey. We might see bright blue for the present and then darker shades of red to violet for likely and less likely futures, until some of them are barely visible in the dark. Totally invisible futures are conceivable but where everything is possible, who's to say.

To get a handle on the full extent of infinity, we'll need to apply some extra imagination to our achievement thus far. So, when we see our rope of every conceivable reality drifting in that immensely vast scale and we walk or float back for a while, our thick and internally illuminated rope can visibly shrink to less than the thickness of a human hair. If we move back even more, it will ultimately become invisible and then lost in the darkness, because there's no sun or sunlight in infinity and also no up or down.

If you want to engage your spiritual aspect, then contemplate who or what you might really be out there where you can create, then see, then lose and hopefully recover everything, just like that. You are the infinity inside yourself looking at infinity outside and you had no problem moving out beyond the physical fabric of your 'real' self to do so.

That small observation is evidence that you could be a more natural part of eternity than you are of the rope that you just created and then lost inside it. However, be careful not to lose sight of the rope for too long because infinity is no place for the naive. Now, mentally move forward to see the rope materialise and be patient, because you or it may have moved a little while you were reading those last few lines.

'Thin Places' occur where the fibres of our rope are frayed or broken and where a spark from the present has jumped across or along the fibres of time. Just as any section of rope can present an isolated strand to whatever surrounds it at any place or time, the same strand can just as easily touch the brightest but thinnest fibre of the central cord at another random place or time, where a 'present' still smolders undetected.

In our comparatively tiny and physical reality of this present, 'Thin Places' often pose as wilderness areas with little sign of previous human activity, but they invariably exude an attraction which is often narcotic to the spirit within many, though not all of us.

They were first documented by the Celts who arrived in Ireland at or about the same time as the old Ogham Script. The result is that few details of 'Thin Places' seem to have survived. Back then, information was spread by word in poetry, song, music and dance and as a result, much of it was already lost to time before the Celts arrived to archive what they found.

Contrary to common belief, most of Irish and also British human history predates the Celts by margins measured in millennia. The Celts certainly made monumental impacts but ultimately, they simply assimilated into the remnants of the genuinely archaic civilisations that built NewGrange, Stonehenge and countless other cosmically aligned wonders of the truly ancient world. So it's only logical to assume that 'Thin Places' exist everywhere in the world, but since I am the product of Gaelic/Celtic ancestors, I can only relate to what they wrote into my own DNA.

'Thin Places' may ooze undocumented histories, but they can also scream and even rage through the ages to spill congealed and often alternate truths like blood gone cold. They are not to be confused with battlefields cum tourist attractions that reek of collective human pain and anguish. Though, who can say with any real conviction that some warriors or innocents don't still wander those static silent soils.

So, tell me that you've never stumbled across an idyllic spot that you couldn't immediately 'relate' to and I'll have to presume that you seldom get out. Next time you stand in your favourite and probably pristine place far from the madding crowds, be wary of almost invisible coils of water in water, when time mixes with time and a new breeze wafts through stale air. This is how Déjà vu feels and how it smells and sometimes, if you close your eyes you can almost imagine being there, but don't. Unless that is, you're sure that you'll be back where you think you are once you open them up again.

The random duplicity of Déjà vu is the catalyst that brings that strand of a lost or possibly broken past, or maybe an unlikely future into the often unseen and anti-climactic embrace of today, of the here and now. After all, we can't expect to have always had a convenient witness on site to recount one otherwise insignificant day being seamlessly exchanged for another.

The portal opens when that sometimes minuscule part of today coincides precisely with another from yesterday or tomorrow and the two realities momentarily merge. However, no version of the past or future can remain rooted indefinitely in the present, so each strand diverges to resume its slow spiral through the rope and through infinity. Where all possibilities exist, those same strands may someday cross each other again but given the scale of infinity, maybe not.

We've all been bemused by Déjà vu which can be as small as a smell or as big as the day itself. But because the day and especially a summer's day is long, the chance duplication of any thin slice of it becomes increasingly more likely than not. The thing is, Ogham was so unwieldy that the Celts never told us how long it takes for a fault in the ultra-thin membrane of time to rupture and then reseal again, but legends suggest it could all take place in the time it takes to fall through.

It is a fact that where there is big there will always be bigger and even vast, as in infinite. Human vanity also knows no bounds and we consider histories without people to play the leading roles as irrelevant footnotes or quiz trivia. Yet, when plate tectonics slowed down to shape our now familiar world, Destiny raised the equivalent of beacons to ensure the success of ensuing Genesis.

These are extraordinarily wild 'Thin Places' made practically inaccessible by design. Such splendid isolation offers greater protection for the desperate and innocently pure, who would populate the earth before any species or tribe could lay claim to being favoured by their creators. These thinnest of all 'Thin Places' are extremely few and so very far between. They are strategically placed at the junctions of ocean and air currents and at the corners of continents so that life and light might flourish for as long as time still burns through the rope of time. On and around them there was never a shortage of nourishment, nor places to rest for exhausted, desperate and sometimes dying swimmers, soarers and sailors.

Once revitalised, these original pioneers could then access new footholds beyond, but on whose shores they would otherwise have been washed up dead or forever lost in time, their flames expired.

To the thinnest place in Ireland, Déjà vu is also a state of mind and the portal through the membrane's veneer lies locked against contamination. It is however, especially porous to the pure and innocent. To those who are also desperately endangered, access to a sanctuary as lofty as the purest ideal is as simple as stumbling through.

Ignatius Moloney didn't care what day it was when he silently set out from Portmagee with his counsellor and carer, but he was trained to automatically retain small details and he knew it was Thursday. In Ogham Gaelic however, Thursday is Deardaoin and so called because in an age largely lost, it lies sandwiched between the day of the first fast, Ceadaoin and the all-day fast of Aoine, now Friday.

Such convenience could be considered good planning for two men of god, dogmatically obliged to observe fasting, except that Ignatius never spoke Gaelic. He was the prime product of select Jesuit Colleges and retreats from Ireland to Rome and back, summa cum laude, fluent in Latin, Greek and Philosophy but lately, a heretic priest.

With two boats bobbing patiently on the gentle swell between theirs and the tiny quay that would be their landing point, the Skipper opted to take his somewhat silently overawed passengers around the rock to make use of some stark light and shadow photo opportunities. Reverend Father Ignatius didn't seem to notice being suddenly deprived of bright sunshine when they were plunged into the monolith's dark and chilly shadow but that was normal.

While his fellow passengers pulled up zips and collars, his gaze remained fixed yet unfocused on whatever patch of sea lay dead ahead. His eyes were in stark contrast to the incessant movement of lips giving form to constant litanies and prayers that weren't always silent.

He grimaced however, when time passed and they were once again exposed to the oblique autumn sun suspended just above a colossal jagged peak. Like Skellig stabbing the sky, the sunlight pierced his irises to obliterate all dark corners, shattering a melancholy so deep that Ignatius had long accepted it as the penance of madness. Face averted and eyes snapped shut, he was left with the disquieting after-image of a gigantic unworldly beacon. But his singular smile grew when a waft of warm welcomes reached out to touch his tortured soul.

PROLOGUE

Charles Iwutchukwu was a living lesson on why no book should ever be judged by its cover. His parents both spoke with Nigerian/English accents and in an idiom that impeccably isolated each syllable, while his own identified him as a human hybrid from inner city Dublin. His adoption by its north-central streets was conditional on using a vernacular laden with slang and delivered in rapid staccato bursts, much like an angry Kalashnikov assault rifle.

It was inevitable that he would eventually bring his street-speak home, which conferred two constants on his already bewildered mother. The first was a deeply furrowed brow that always preceded the second, which was a question of just one word, usually delivered in a rising crescendo, 'WHAT?'.

There was no doubting the proud pedigree of his west african blood but his heart was pure emerald. So much so, that a select and tightly knit band of college friends considered him to be the darkest Irishman since Bram Stoker. Charles' Jesuit sponsored degree in psychology and counselling might have once seemed a singularly unlikely achievement, but his deeply ingrained sense of belonging demanded an equally compelling empathy for like minded souls.

When Dublin County was the first and only 'Pale' his first name might have been less of a burden, but even a hundred years after the rebellion that broke the back of the British Empire, it wasn't a tag worn easily. What he needed was a derivative that didn't totally disregard his parents best intentions, but also something with a more parochial flavour. So, Chaz was how he chose to be known as he set about cultivating his own unique brand of himself. Years later, he was still Chaz to the Jesuit Brotherhood, for whom the name raised many eyebrows but no objections as his nom du guerre.

Chaz wasn't a priest and he harboured no intentions of becoming one, but he wore his 'Clerical Brother's' black cassock whenever he was out and about, even though it could be quite dangerous. He towered over most men and was afraid of none, but there was little distinction between his clothes and his dark complexion. It was a potentially lethal combination that made him almost invisible on nighttime streets.

To him, the garb was his officer's unmarked uniform. It bore no rank chevrons or shoulder epaulettes to identify him as a high grade target engaged on battlefields of the mind. His special-ops training made him all things to all men so he could get them safely back behind friendly lines to plan the next sortie. Always fresh in his mind, an oath to never leave any behind.

The outfit was also a shield that hid occasional sins of presumption on preferential treatment to get his many missions accomplished. The short notice acquisition of two Skellig tickets that others would need to book a month in advance, was a case in point. In an increasingly material world, Chaz wasn't afraid to admit that even the soldiers of Jesus needed all the help they could get.

However, he surprised himself by how easily he fell victim to the infusion of unease. Skellig day trips still featured high on the bucket lists of gullible star-faring nerds, but he may as well have been one of them just then. The only thing that stopped him from adding his own to so many skyward gazes, suspecting alien causes for the abrupt change of ambience, was the call of duty. He was reassured by the sight of his companion, who was really his charge standing as motionless as he'd left him. The Reverend Father Ignatius seemed pretty much oblivious to everything, even the sudden chill.

Just what the Jedi-junkies expected to see in the sky above them was anyone's guess, but Chaz felt he should have been above such impulsive apprehensions. A trained Jesuit was automatically blessed with dominion over all things supernatural and that faith based logic quickly prevailed. However, his flesh and blood aspect obliged him to isolate the components of a natural phenomena that could spawn such potent xenophobia.

Firstly, the clouds were not one thing or the other. They were a strangely layered mix of leaden, patchy and thin, which produced glaringly bright holes where the sun threatened to burst through. And when it did, a very strange stage was set. Time of day then collaborated perfectly with the sun's angle to produce intensely sharp contrasts of light and shadow, of warmth and chill. Moving from one to the other was enough to apparently transform day into dusk, like an unscheduled solar eclipse.

Mere moments before, his fellow passengers shared the camaraderie of tolerant tourist smiles that belied the fact that most were already in mild discomfort. Most were either too warm or too confined under intermittent but potent sunlight and bulky life-vests worn over water and/or windproof jackets. Prominent red-lettered signs did enough to discourage the removal of vests and periodic squinting was becoming tiresome.

Bright sunlight from above can be irritating, but when it's also reflected from a shimmering sea alongside, the only option for relief is to turn away. However, on the other side of the boat, natural formations of gigantic gothic rock cathedrals seemed to harvest all the light received and then throw it back in their admirers' faces. The glare was such that despite innate curiosity, little detail could be discerned from inside the comparatively ink-black cracks of countless crevices and fissures.

Lastly, latent human frailties can surface in response to the mystical power of places like Skellig. Rising anticipation of imminent physical contact with the oldest and therefore the holiest of holy Irish monastic sites complemented an increased charge to the subordinate 'Jedi Force' aspect. So when their world was plunged into comparative darkness, intuitive human fears from darker ages raised more than goosebumps and neck hair.

To Chaz, everything came together so quickly that it made an absolute mockery of 'so called' twenty-first century civilisation. He saw its ultra-thin veneer shatter as the prospect of divine retribution subliminally cultivated over more than two thousand years and/or countless Star-Wars episodes burst through the clouds.

Hot on the heels of that minor revelation came the more mundane observation that the existence of a circuit breaker is academic until something trips it, to accord it supreme significance. So when the boat literally dropped out of sunlight to apparently disappear into the deep shadow of Skellig Michael, even his first thought was of prayer. His second concerned the Reverend Father Ignatius, who could sometimes be as helpless as a child.

Chaz hid behind his black superhero cloak as it predictably parted small knots of passengers that made up the dozen or so accompanying them that day. This allowed him to glide over the deck to where Ignatius peered dead ahead over the prow. As gently as he could, he placed a hand on the priest's shoulder to remind him that he wasn't alone and then just as quickly, the boat popped up on a swell and the sun came out again.

Ignatius responded to the dual touches of hand and laser like sunshine by slowly turning towards him. Chaz waited for a consistently confused face, accompanied as always by an adulterated blend of assorted sacramental and ceremonial prayers, always in latin. Some minutes before, he'd left him with his Litany of the Saints after suffering through futile prayers for the sick and the dying, but the priest's mouth was unexpectedly still.

Ignatius offered only silence and a face far too white. It beamed brilliantly but with eyes somehow forced painfully open to admit the glorious glare. He was enraptured by Skellig's apparently blazing pinnacle high above his puzzled protector.

Chaz took his turn to mumble his own prayer of gratitude for the serenity so unexpectedly bestowed on the tormented priest, while the boat turned for the now vacated landing site. Beyond that ecstatic face, Chaz glimpsed the curiosity of what looked like a surfacing penguin with an extraordinary thick bill. A tiny black bead of an eye in a large white eyepatch regarded him cautiously and then dived. Stunted black wings then blurred into action as they propelled it, torpedo like towards Skellig.

“Saved.” Said the priest with a whisper, his eyes expanding as if seeing Chaz for the very first time. Then he clasped the tall brother’s right hand in both of his and pumped it gratefully, like a self confessed murderer inexplicably acquitted by the jury.

Ignatius then filled the silence while Chaz looked for some bearings in the unfamiliar territory of being totally lost for words.

“I can’t thank you enough for rescuing me Brother.” But his eyes had already moved beyond his dark superhero to drink in more of Skellig.

1 - AWAKENED

"Father Ignatius. You need to slow down and adjust to where we are." He gulped down another lungful of air before he was able to say more.

"You may not fully realise it yet, but there are vegetables that have been better company than you these last few months and then suddenly, you're the man with the mission. If you don't need to get acclimated to the new you that's fine, but I'm having problems with it. So, let's stop and talk about this for a little while." Chaz was proof that larger bodies consume more energy than smaller ones and especially when forced to catch up on an incline. However, Ignatius seemed to take his dark brother's proximity as an irritation and a cue to move on even faster.

"My name is Ignatius, Chaz. I'm not reverend any more, so just call me Ignatius for god's sake." Ignatius threw the words behind him without bothering to see where they fell and equally oblivious to the somewhat blasphemous irony they held.

He stopped about fifty meters from Blind Man's Cove, where they'd just come onshore. The jeans and anorak clad priest was studiously examining the rock wall on his right, as if looking for some weakness through which he might see more of the underlying nature of Skellig. Apparently not finding what he was looking for, he took off again but this time at a run and without the handicap of a small backpack hanging from each shoulder, unlike Chaz. Ignatius only had eyes for the rock towering above them, like hearing a voice that he just then recognised but in a language he couldn't.

Chaz had first begun to realise the priest might not be fully recovered from his mental malaise when, totally out of character, he pushed past him to leap directly from the boat rail onto Skellig's tiny quay. He'd also done it out of turn, which meant he came close to colliding with a fellow passenger who wasn't yet clear of the lower steps.

Fortunately, he stuck where he landed, like cotton meeting a velcro patch. Then, without a backward glance, he was on top of the small pier and jogging along the pebble crunching pathway towards the lighthouse. But because he wasn't the first to disembark, he was soon obliged to squeeze through the first of two small groups of fellow passengers who'd adopted a default, leisurely day-trip pace. Chaz saw him mutter what he could only assume were apologies, but Ignatius didn't hang around to see if they were well received. He just kept going.

That sudden burst of well coordinated agility from a man previously capable of minimal cognitive processing had caught Chaz completely off guard. As he hauled his bigger bulk onto the pier and into pursuit of his fleet-footed patient, he was obliged to reflect on the nature of that apparently miraculous recovery.

The reasons why Ignatius had taken his untimely sabbatical from the divinely dominated world weren't complex, but they were profound enough to completely alter his personality. When Chaz sought the highly considered opinion of his own mentor, he was told that the chances of such a dramatic recovery were virtually nil.

Summer had literally flown past but Chaz remembered only too well how this chapter began. He received the startling surprise of a personal summons by the new Irish Provincial to receive new orders and duly arrived at the superior's plush office with an apprehension not unlike that of a schoolboy being summoned to the headmaster's office. He knew the man had spent most of his life either studying or teaching in one or the other of Europe's elite Jesuit colleges, and he certainly looked the part, which did little to put Chaz at ease.

His clumps of thick grey hair were long enough to suggest someone who didn't hold vanity or barbers in high regard and his eyes when they met his, were a little too steady to be friendly. However, having apparently passed some unstated inspection, the superior's demeanour quickly changed and a smile slowly sprouted on a face that was subtly transformed into its opposite. His firm handshake was much warmer than the room.

After that first impersonal appraisal, the Irish Provincial began to show him hints of doctor, academic, polished politician and seasoned authoritarian. He was a man who could comment on anything and miss nothing, not even the small involuntary shiver that rippled through the big brother's substantial frame.

Then, just as quickly, it was business. Chaz was casually informed that the central heating was turned down to ensure it would still be available for a really cold day. Traces of his exhaled breath hung in the chilled air, but he thought better of possibly appearing soft in front of a man who was old enough to maybe feel the cold more than he should. So he simply nodded with words to the effect that everyone should do more to reduce their carbon footprints.

People who live and work in closed or tight communities tend to be better communicators than those who would call them gossips, and he'd already heard of the unfortunate Father Ignatius Moloney. Chaz was qualified in the workings of the human mind, but he found that his own could confuse him almost as much as others did. To keep himself objective and far removed from his patients, he found that he worked better by filing.

He began by mentally filing people in folders of their own names and his first input was a small list of essential, though largely generic information. Then he would add colour coded subfolders, green to purple for each major discovery and was duly obliged to add a sub-folder of tragedies. That purple subfolder was quickly filled with subsequent purple sub-folders detailing each disaster to befall their damaged priest.

It transpired that his rather unusual name was given to the priest as a child. It wasn't personally adopted out of reverence for the Jesuit founding Father, Ignatius Loyola. As he stood there on the polished wooden floor and hands behind his back, like a soldier standing at ease, he remembered wondering just how many Jesuits were actually called Ignatius. Meanwhile, the Provincial had already begun listing the outline contents of each tragedy subfolder.

Ignatius had a brother called William, who was only a few years older but who died of a heart attack only a month after the priest's ordination. It happened during a family Mass that his mother had asked him to perform as part of her special request. She was so proud of him.

The superior believed that it was because Ignatius had put so much effort into suppressing his grief instead of suffering with it, that he lost some of his previously enviable focus. He started mixing the words of the two sacraments he subsequently administered that day. The first was the Mass commemorating the sacrifice of Jesus, which was interrupted at a crucial stage so he could perform the Last Rites and offer comfort to the dead and dying, his brother. He later tended to slip in and out of the latin versions, which wasn't always appropriate in public.

Ignatius' father was already quite frail and he took the loss of his eldest son quite badly. When he passed away so soon afterwards, his mother was devastated and had to be taken into care. The old wive's tale of disasters coming in threes, came to pass plus one, when his sister was later diagnosed with breast cancer. God's apparent abandonment of his newly ordained priest setting out on a life of dedicated service made absolutely no sense to Ignatius, and so he reciprocated in kind.

Because of the many functions it has evolved to fulfil the Jesuit Order is largely self sufficient, with the result that the Provincial had no shortage of in-house options to choose from. After relieving the Reverend Father Ignatius of his duties, he placed him in the care of Brother Chaz, with a mission to nurture him back to a semblance of mental, physical and spiritual health. Chaz was given priority access to any and all Jesuit medical and educational institutions to augment his own expertise and he was ordered to report monthly.

Not long out of training, Chaz was already cutting his teeth amongst the desperate and suicidal, whether drug and/or alcohol addicted misfits or maladjusted youth of callous Ireland. He seized this new assignment as a vote of confidence in his abilities but, when he was introduced to Ignatius and the enormity of the task assailed him, his enthusiasm flagged. The priest was capable of breathing and a pulse could occasionally be seen rising a vein. He also ate sometimes but slept little and Chaz likened him to a mental zombie, psychologically and spiritually deceased.

Chaz had to dig deep inside himself to re-ignite the spiritual warrior that he'd so thinly spread over the streets of Dublin. Guided further by his Jesuit pseudo military assimilation, he immersed himself in Examen to purge himself of selfish disappointments and took the bit between his teeth for a stricken comrade in arms.

Chaz patiently prodded the priests damaged psyche but any apparent improvement was too brief to be clinically defined as such, and was usually followed by relapse. Knowing that failure would soon see Ignatius committed to a dedicated specialist facility, Chaz was growing desperate for a solution and dedicated a separate Examen to finding a solution and this one lasted days.

Examen is a process whereby challenges are broken down into their smallest components to facilitate micro-management. Properly done, macro solutions can be simultaneously applied to problems that would otherwise appear insurmountable. He discovered that the fundamental requirement was for him to meet like with like. Physical damage could be offset by physical repairs like rest and therapy, but a damaged spirit was in need of something else.

Religion invariably entertains spiritual dimensions from where esoteric entities like angels, jinn and even demons can be either summoned or are unnaturally innate. So it struck

Chaz that since Ignatius' condition was too complex to have a clinically defined cause, it was beyond any of his textbook solutions. Ignatius was a priest who had a critically damaged spiritual psyche and the only prescription was spiritual renewal. The problem was that his patient refused prayer and could no longer acknowledge that divinity played any role in his life.

From long before the dark ages, Skellig Michael had a reputation throughout Western Europe and beyond for ascetic spiritual renewal. That renown had blossomed into a virtually universal acclaim through some superb cinematic appeal and scripts of epic, extra-galactic proportions. It was now a magnet for theist, secular and even atheists in search of their 'Force'. So Chaz couldn't help but wonder at how much more effective it could be for a dedicated man of god, if he could just get him to pray from its ancient dedicated monastery.

The total elation he experienced on finding Father Ignatius miraculously returned to the land of the living and before they'd even set foot on Skellig was all but gone. Something was seriously wrong but it wasn't until the lighthouse pathway swung left under a protective canopy to take them around Cross Cove, that he caught up with his more athletic companion.

The leading group of fellow excursionists were in for a shock when the previously affable african, with the demeanour and outward appearance of a foreign priest, suddenly body tackled a random and regular guy. Chaz had grown tired of jogging uphill and caught Ignatius in a bear hug, but was still required to use his weight as an anchor and to stop a very determined man in his tracks.

With his patient safely constrained, Chaz needed to reassure everyone that he was wasn't a mugger in fancy dress. 'Black Lives Matter' had evolved into something more global.

"I'm afraid my friend here can occasionally suffer some severe autistic lapses and that's when I have to stop him running off and maybe getting himself hurt." Like everything Jesuit, it was said with a practised ease that made it almost glib. He'd chosen it from his repertoire of pre-prepared contingency plans and as such, it was delivered with convincing confidence.

"And he's going up there?" Asked a tall lanky young man with another, though younger jeans, jacket and back-pack guy nodding in agreement. The speaker was pointing in the general direction of the South Steps, just then obscured by the section of cliff wall at the head of Cross Cove.

Chaz smiled, his teeth looking even more like a dentist's advert against the contrast of his black face. "Don't you worry about Ignatius here. I'll just have a quiet talk with him and if need be, I'll put him back on his leash." The group of four hesitated for just a moment but then fell victim to the cleric's contagious laughter.

Then, more seriously, "- In case you're worried about any of this, I'm also a doctor and Ignatius is a patient of mine," offered Chaz conspiratorially. They nodded in unison, accepting the subliminal invitation to keep a secret with a priest, who just happened to be a doctor who looked as capable as any Sumo wrestler. What could be more convincing?

"Chaz. Let me go Chaz. You're forgetting that I'm the priest here."

That brought some quizzical looks to the bystanders' faces and Chaz gave them a 'and-you-thought-your-job-was-difficult-look' in return. The big man then released his captive slowly but in phases. First loosening the vise-grip around his upper torso, then freeing an arm, then another one and so on. Ignatius was progressively released while their fellow day-trippers waited to see if he would accept his fate. It was only when he voluntarily faced up the big man that they turned away and left them to resolve their doctor-patient or priest-penitent differences in private.

Chaz had to speak louder than he would have liked. Skellig was the epitome of pristine isolation, but it was far from quiet with a constant racket from squabbling birds in particular.

“The Provincial has grounded you Ignatius, so you can’t pull rank on me and you must know that I can’t let you run around here like a lunatic. I don’t like it any more than you do, but I’m responsible for you and I only brought you here because I couldn’t possibly have anticipated your sudden … lucidity. I thought we would be taking it together and that I’d have to practically carry you up to the monastery, but I was very happy to do that for you. But if you insist on getting ahead of me like that again, we’ll have to stay down here and just miss out on the monastery, sad as that may be for both of us and a huge waste of our allowances to boot.”

Ignatius took a minute but lost only a fraction of his ‘crazy’ look. So, Chaz waited until they were alone again, nodding nonchalantly to the inevitable stragglers who’d caught up with them and then passed them by.

“I’m sorry Chaz, but it’s like I’ve been sleepwalking and I’ve just woken up to the fact that there’s a reason why I’m here. I’m also sure that reason might be waiting for me up there somewhere.” Ignatius was pointing further along the pathway.

“You’re looking at that reason, Father Ignatius. It was my idea, though I will admit to a little help from the Holy Spirit but in any case, the direction you’re pointing doesn’t go very far.”

Chaz took him by the arm until they rounded the southernmost Cross Cove outcrop together. From there it was less than a hundred metres to the point at which the South-Steps separated from the lighthouse pathway. They were set into a steep slope of heather, grass and scree between two sections of near vertical cliff. In fact, the first few steps were so steep that a couple of switchbacks was built into them before they could rise in the general direction of the monastic settlement.

However, one look at Ignatius told him that the priest's main point of interest was indeed much further along the pathway. He was looking at the furthest promontory rocks where the lighthouse buildings stood.

"Do you see the construction worker's pre-fabs and the covered section of pathway just beyond the steps?" Chaz didn't wait for an answer.

"Well, there's a lot of work still to be done up there to make that part of Skellig safe, so it's strictly out of bounds. Besides, to get to the monastery we'll need to take those steps," said pointing to the Southern Steps, "- and that's why everyone is assembling there for the safety briefing. If we don't get that briefing we risk being told to stay down here for our own good. Is that what you want?" Chaz struggled to hold the deepest furrows his broad forehead could support.

Ignatius seemed to settle just a little, though his neck might have been a swivel on which his head swung between his formidable clerical companion and a point somewhere beyond the Blue Man's Rock, like he was trying to locate someone who'd gone on ahead of him.

"Anyway. What could be up that end of the track that's more important than the monastery above us?" Chaz offered a huge hand to the priest, who knew that taking it would also be accepting an obligation to follow his guide's instructions.

He tried to explain his reluctance. "You don't understand Chaz. There is a hell of a lot more to this place than first meets the eye, though trying to describe is as difficult as explaining colour to a blind man. There's a presence with a source, or maybe that's better described as a source with a presence. Anyway, I must find it, so why can't we meet up later at the monastery?" He put his palms together as he would in earnest prayer, except there was something too pitiful and even desperate about it. Then he took a small step backwards, testing his virtual leash.

Chaz pondered the situation. It was very positive that Ignatius was in tune with his surroundings and was less of the wide eyed lunatic, though his arguments were illogical. The problem for his guardian was that to everyone else on Skellig, Ignatius looked like just another tourist. Chaz could probably wrangle his way further along the track, but Ignatius wouldn't get the preferential treatment that he could normally expect as a priest with a robe and collar. In fact, he would probably find himself forcibly removed from Skellig and put back on the boat for persistently straying off the beaten track. That was if he was lucky enough not to kill himself first.

The pre-eminent feeling that Chaz had for Skellig just then, was of an accident waiting to happen and he was beginning to regret taking Ignatius over.

"Maybe we should just forget about Skellig and what it means to you for just a few minutes, so we can talk about how you suddenly snapped out of a melancholia that had you spouting nothing but latin gibberish for months on end."

But a thought struck Chaz as the last of those words met the pristine Atlantic air. What if Father Ignatius was also being led by the spirit, and it was he who was obstructing a mysteriously divine purpose?

So he continued more carefully. "I think the Holy Spirit can only take you to one place on Skellig Michael, Father Ignatius. So, why don't we say a small prayer together for further guidance on the matter?" Chaz bent his head, inviting Ignatius to join him and then closed his eyes in concentration.

Ignatius was somewhere on the journey back to being a priest, a somewhat irreverent one as it happened, but there was still some protocols to be observed. So, Chaz waited for the ranking cleric to begin. But when his ears only received the all pervasive chorus of a hundred thousand sea birds and the steady shush of waves on rocks alongside, he decided to forgo etiquette and take the lead himself. He opened his eyes to confirm that Father Ignatius was ready but he only saw his back, by then burrowing through the company of assembled tourists.

The group was being addressed by a man perched on the first few steps above them. He wore a typical construction worker's hard hat but was interrupted by the more commanding voice of Chaz, loud even from a distance. Once he looked, they were all drawn to the voice that was roaring after the priest.

"Ignatius! Wait!"

Chaz was infuriated to see all faces directed at him and not one following the man that they all saw him physically restrain only minutes before. "Stop him for God's sake."

When the penny dropped, one or two of them swung around to look in the other direction, but Ignatius was already inside the half tunnel of the covered section of track and running hard towards the worker's pre-fabs and the lighthouse beyond.

"Bollox." Roared Chaz, reverting to a native dialect that his Jesuit education and training had almost convinced him he'd never used.

Ignatius sprinted through a clutter of stones and rocks, some of them surprisingly large, that had fallen out of the cliffs to lie scattered along the restricted stretch of pathway. The curved roofing exaggerated the sound of his occasional contact with debris, but the even louder sounds of pursuit spurred him on without looking back.

The lighthouse pathway was wound around the girth of Skellig like a small ribbon falling higher and higher as it got closer to the functioning lighthouse, and even higher again towards the older ruined lighthouse at the end of the track. If two other ribbons marked the steeper, easterly and northerly access routes to the comparatively level saddle shaped rest area, where they met the ribbon of the southern steps. Then the overall impression would be that of a clear wrapped uncut diamond set into an aquamarine sea, but only on a clear day. On most days, it would simply be obscured by clouds.

The relentless incline slowed Ignatius until all he could manage was a breathless fast walk on the uneven ribbon that would take him past the lighthouse. There were ten labourers and two supervisors on Skellig that day, but most of them were much higher up on the extreme isolation of the treacherous terraces on the South Peak. Two more were just finishing a minor repair to the South Steps that everyone except Ignatius and Chaz would be shortly using. That left one yellow headed supervisor who was tasked with the safety briefing, but who'd just joined Chaz in the pursuit of his perturbed priest.

Jimmy McGuire was the tenth Office of Public Works labourer on duty, and was loudly cursing the thickness of a hole drilled through the wall at the back of the automated lighthouse facility. Clenched in a grimy hand was the now well-scuffed end of a communications cable from a satellite dish discreetly hidden amongst the rocks overlooking the compound. His problem was the obvious disparity between the thickness of cable and that of the hole drilled on a previous day.

The initial solution of trying to force the cable through the existing hole was always unlikely, given the thickness of a wall built when budgets weren't so miserly. So he rose with rheumatoid reluctance from his knees to his feet and then slowly stretched an aching back. Jimmy had also taken one cup of tea too many with his corned beef sandwich and he also needed to relieve himself of it.

Multitasking was never a McGuire strong point, so he opted to defer the problem of the cable. That left him free to satisfy nature's call while expressing his displeasure at such mediocre Office of Public Works planning. He proceeded to mark the offending wall with his scent, and in so doing was reminded of a dog he once knew. However, he was interrupted mid-flow by the sound of shoes sliding on gravel somewhere behind him.

"How in hell did he get all the way up here without being stopped?" He muttered under his breath at the sight of a younger man sashaying from one side of the path to the other, like he was drunk or something. The idiot was headed further up the pathway towards the ruins of the old lighthouse.

From being mildly upset, Jimmy was now angry because the tourist was almost upon a vertical fifty metre drop into Seal's Cove and a winter storm had taken out the sea wall, along with a bite shaped slice of pathway.

He was caught between stashing his private's back into his pants and stopping the madman.

"HEY YOU!"

A startled face looked back at a man who was fighting with his zipper while apparently shouting obscenities.

"Where do you think you're goin'?" Jimmy threw out the challenge using his best Dingle brogue.

Ignatius was not inclined to swap inane banter with an extremely gruff looking individual, who coincidentally looked like he might be harbouring some possibly questionable motives, so he took off uphill. He knew that Chaz would most likely have enlisted the help of others who wouldn't be far behind, but he felt he was closer to his objective.

He couldn't describe it as a physical attraction but calling it metaphysical would be to underestimate something that was pulling him inside out, so he chanced one last glance over his shoulder. This would confirm the quality of the pursuit so he could keep them at a distance but without burning himself out in the process. Ignatius couldn't have chosen a worse time to take his eyes off the pathway.

In a way, it was extremely fortunate that he was running when he went over the edge. That's because his forward momentum gave him a trajectory that offered a chance, however slim, of clearing the cliff wall as he fell. He hadn't realised just how high above the waves he'd climbed and for just a moment, Ignatius felt he was floating like a gull caught on the updrafts. He had time enough to start working on the mathematics of how long his fall would take from what looked like fifty metres give or take. A nominal acceleration rate of ten metres per second per second offered itself up for inclusion in the formula, which was just then being complicated by more gusts.

The answer had almost elapsed when the incidental figure of his final velocity alerted him to the more urgent requirement of avoiding a belly flop while hitting water. He'd fallen from high enough to break his back or neck or both, so at that very last moment he twisted his body catlike, and then pushed out his arms before him. He ended up facing a cliff wall much darker than it was higher up. It was covered increasingly with guano, then limpets, sea-weeds and finally, with spray.

It was also far too close and Ignatius was astonished at how calmly he was taking everything when water slapped him painfully in the face and then engulfed his being. His mouth and eyes automatically snapped shut, but there was so much going on in his head that shock was retarded, though he did register immense pressure following the initial impact. He arched his back in an attempt at pull out of the dive in reverse to clear of the submerged cliff, while also anticipating a bone-crunching jar of failure to do so. But he met nothing until his hands felt something cold and slick.

When he opened his eyes, Ignatius was suspended within the brown branches of tall kelp trees undulating to the dance of invisible submarine waves. The clear bright day of above was replaced by an iridescent imprecision in everything from the middle to longer distances. Close up however, a dark penguin with a white belly and a small black eye in a large white eyepatch flashed into view, and then stilled its stunted winglets to coast slowly closer until it stopped.

"But there are no penguins in Ireland …" - he mused, getting the distinct impression that the unlikely creature was as puzzled by him as he was with it. With a speed he considered impossible through water, the creature presented a gaping yellow mouth to his face before apparently choosing to chomp instead on his hand. With a pressure more appropriate to that of a pit-bull terrier, its thick serrated beak slashed painfully through skin until he felt it scrape against bone.

The sight of his own blood welling out to form delicate red streamers in the water around him was enough to take him halfway out of his stupor, and the belated arrival of shock did the rest. In less than a millisecond, he was able to relive the insanity of an adrenaline induced survival instinct that took him so far from the reality of what should have been his death plunge. His out of body experience ended and his mind re-engaged with his anatomy to return both to the authority of his own reckless devices. Then he made another fatal mistake by gasping at a considerable depth of water.

2 - UWAG-NAS

Despite maintaining a fairly constant depth except to take an occasional breath, the ambience of bottomless ocean began to change. Out of the gloom, diffuse shades and colours became sharp enough to form a three dimensional rock and vegetation strewn sea-floor, which rose to meet her. That increased detail beneath, combined with the much anticipated spike in water temperature to announce shallows. Shallow however, is a rather relative term and for Uwag-Nas, who could dive to depths of perpetual darkness and traverse entire oceans, it meant imminent salvation or doom but ultimately, destiny.

She was not a migrant by nature and the longest journey ever taken was finally over, though just then she feared it may have taken her more time than she had. She'd invested so much of it that going back home, though always futile, was now unlikely. The most beautiful, capable and intelligent by far of her diminished tribe would probably live and die alone and as far from family and friends as it was possible to be.

The last of the three great havens were once considered inviolable, but it seemed that only the waters around Sunset Haven still carried the scent of her kind, though only just. She'd discovered to her great dismay that Aurora Haven was practically barren. Now, despite the benign credentials of Sunrise Haven and shoals of silver sprats laid on as welcome gifts, she could neither hear nor smell any signs of her kind. There was also a really bad omen in the form of a Dyb-Bok flotilla idling on the waves offshore.

Genetic memory strong enough to spawn this greatest adventure carried with it the solemn oath to stay hidden from Dyb-Bok, but the demons didn't look like dispersing anytime soon and there was nowhere else to go. To maintain her now instinctive stealth, Uwag-Nas had no choice but to approach Sunrise Haven from its opposite side and dove deeper to work her way around.

Sound carries better through the water universe than it does through that of land and sky, and even though she no longer saw it, she heard one of the noisy sputtering things separate from its flock while she raced under the waves. It slowly circled Sunrise Haven at a distance that made it impossible for her to stay safe. Intentionally or otherwise, it was blocking her final approach. So, with no choice but to stand off and wait longer, she accepted more sprats. She felt fatigued enough to consider surrender but after so long at sea, she was also svelte and well muscled.

A glint from a sky-shark's blue green skin below, together with the realisation that she was almost within touching distance of the last of the Great Havens, forced a difficult decision on her. A large seal could take a sky-shark if it was hungry and fast enough, and she could certainly smell seals in the water, but the last of a kind daren't dally with death.

Alert to the new threat, she returned to optimum depth. The stalking predator didn't need to see her sleek silhouette slide across the sea-sky ceiling above, though it did. Those eyes and ears were augmented with electromagnetic radar to provide independent triangulation and a precise location, even at night.

Uwag-Nas had survived the vastness of the broad Storm Ocean, losing the protection of her father to much bigger jaws along the way and evolution obliged her to learn fast from that encounter. So, drawing closer to the surface, she waited like bait until the white flash of teeth. That would be the instant in which the shark would commit to the results of its tracking and targeting.

She twisted and simultaneously shot out of the sea universe into the other of sky, but did so with such speed and agility that she stayed aloft longer than her pursuer could anticipate, while also changing direction. The sky-shark would chomp on an empty space and then again on a projected space, only to dive deep with nothing to show for a normally successful strategy.

Uwag-Nas erred however in being over absorbed with the isolated threat and lost track of the circling Dyb-Bok, some of whom had seen her long distance leap. She was constantly alert to danger because at sea, it lies potentially in all seven dimensions. In time immemorial, her kind had left the sea for land as a very different species, and then walked for long enough to leave the land universe and to fly in the third, only to come full circle and return to the sea. She was the mistress of all three universes and so, missed absolutely nothing in any of them.

In a jump transformed by adopting a genetically recalled profile providing aerodynamic lift, she caught far more details of the Dyb-Bok than they could of her. That was especially true of the closest but strangely passive Dyb-Bok, who seemed preoccupied with something in the far distance and as a result was no threat. But the giant one with all black plumage had made unmistakable eye contact. So she dived vertically on re-entering the water, compelled to risk following the sky-shark into the depths.

Lungs replenished, she soon sighted the undulating animal angling harmlessly away but dived deeper still. She was told again and again that Dyb-Bok could call upon occult powers of entrapment and since she'd already been observed, she would need to stay submerged for as long as she could. The last of the Great Havens called her down and then further down and then showed her a safe place to hide.

The submerged archway looked like it might have been carved out by sea-level waves, though in an epoch beyond all living memory. It expanded to embrace her as she simultaneously closed on the walls of Haven just beyond. Once inside, Uwag-Nas intended to gently float to the roof and rest there until the Dyb-Bok peril passed. Expressed in something other than digits, she used an age old formula that converted energy and air conserved into time submerged and therefore semi-safe.

With eyes as keen as her sense of smell and depth perception, she froze when the water shimmered around her, but when no stealthy shadows edged furtively closer, she pushed cautiously on. The slightly sparkling phenomena was so subtle that she wondered if it could be simply a novelty of sunlight through living water, a transitory vacuous veil woven from refraction and roving shadow.

She felt nothing swimming through the mirror image of the almost same sea behind her. Beyond it however, the archway morphed into a longer tunnel. There was still plenty of light at the end of it, but it was the light of another day. The prime directive of avoiding Dyb-Bok at all costs drove her on. So, she warily swam a stretch of tunnel that was longer than it first appeared, though she thought better of lingering inside a structure likely to shift shape again.

Uwag-Nas cautiously emerged to see that it wasn't just the ambient light that had changed. Her ears also picked up some unexpected variations. The Dyb-Bok gurgling had totally disappeared, but there was a manifold increase to the natural raucousness above the sea-sky interface that more than compensated. Only a gradual ascent would tell her why daylight had dulled so quickly and also the reason behind a surge in sea-sky sounds. As a clumsy creature on land and more so on unfamiliar rocks, she would need to find the comparative safety of deeper water or better still, a beach if there was a storm on the wind.

Climbing through a kelp forest as tall as any she'd seen on her long travels, the last thing she expected to come across was a dead Dyb-Bok. She'd never seen one up close before but since dead things are just food for scavengers, she paused for a closer look and maybe to learn something from it. Unlike her naive ancestors, she was unnaturally curious to know what it was that made the beasts so dangerous.

She recognised it as the passive creature with no eyes for Uwag-Nas and since it never posed a threat, even while alive, she was bold enough to draw closer. She could move very fast, but the change was so rapid that she had to blink to register any movement at all. In a single frame of frozen life, its eyes had gone from sealed by death to opened wide and also locked onto hers, so she struck out hard.

The devil was covered with a second and maybe even a third layer of skin, except on the head and at the tip of its stubby wings. But since heads will always hold teeth, she slashed at a wingtip with her strong grooved razorbill. When she cut it straight through to the bone, the apparent fragility of a beast that was lethal beyond legend, came as a surprise to ingest.

However, instinct whipped her out of indecision with an automatic flight response. Tackling such a potent predator would normally be an act of desperation and a last resort, but having already struck, she switched on speed to escape. As she was about to flee, the damaged Dyb-Bok released a long black feather that had somehow become entangled in the blunt tips of its other wing.

It was beyond curious that a Dyb-Bok could possess something that she hadn't seen since leaving Sunset Haven and despite herself, she had to have it. As it happened, the devil was leaking blood and also had flight on its mind. Its eyes opened wider and then wider still, while a mouth set into the bottom of its flat face did the same. A torrent of bubbles streamed out between two rows of blunt looking teeth towards the air universe. So, she watched the creature flail frantically while apparently racing its own bubbles upwards. If not for their barbaric history, she could have considered the thing more ugly and clumsy than pitiful.

Turning her prize around in her bill, she caught the thicker stem end and punctured it to release its essence. Smell and taste told the story of a fresh moult from the wing of a young male. His unique oily tang was still strong and she almost flipped for joy.

The feather meant that she'd found a viable colony in Sunrise Haven and it was one in which a breeding season was just completed. No telltale female scent on his feather was a reminder that her own biological clock would not run forever. She couldn't afford to waste a single moment.

On the surface, her objective would be the same as that of any mature female, but hers was a far more primal urge. Finding the feather's owner and then establishing herself as a potential mate would require status. Being by far the most attractive and capable of her kind would normally make that task easy, but this wasn't her colony. There were historical reasons why her kind didn't migrate, and she could expect a particularly hostile reception from the skein leader.

Like life everywhere, Uwag-Nas was primarily driven by impulse and instinct evolved from positive and negative experiences. This complemented genetic memory gleaned from ancient incarnations spent mud-crawling, then walking to eventually culminate in flying, before apparently settling on swimming.

The historical mastery of her kind in each universe invaded, inevitably produced the positive experiences of large populations. But rampant success makes guile redundant to produce naivete and when further change arrived, in the form of new or more capable predators, extinction beckoned. The Dyb-Bok invasions of all but two of the Great Havens changed everything but without them, she would at best be a simple shadow of what she needed to become.

Evolution has just one master, which is the stimulus provided by life itself and it had lately applied itself with atypical avidity on the lost tribe of Uwag-Nas. If they were to survive, some long dormant attributes had to be awakened and their critical complacency lost with new blood lines added. Regardless of whether she lived or died, she was now the only possible future for her kind and if destiny decreed death, then tears were redundant. There never were that many anyway, but whatever was shed were already long dried.

The Great Havens are primal places where original destinies remain impervious to contamination. They are also beacons that call out to evolution's masterpieces and then impartially preside over subsequent meetings. All life needs senses to survive, and a Haven can be located by smell until close enough to positively identify by sight. But from over the horizon and from the darkness of confused or desperate minds, they also call directly to the life force within, in a case of like calling like.

The equivalent of a red tipped needle swivels rises and then falls within each of us as we move through the swells and troughs of life. It's a delicate precision instrument though encased in a solid construction to make it immune to storms, just like a ship's steady compass. It points in directions dictated by some other aspect of life to junctions.

Uwag-Nas was not just the most beautiful, but also the cleverest of her kind and yet, she was still someway behind completion on evolution's production line. She couldn't know just then that Havens are never exclusive. She was just one possible future amongst others being nudged towards rejection, or to impossibly altered destinies.

3 - DOOAH

"Cower!!"

"COWER LAKEYON NISH NISH!!"

"GUVORRAH DAGDA ORRING!"

There was a name at the extreme edge of his recall and Ignatius struggled to put it next to the once familiar, but much fresher face that materialised at the periphery of his imagination. It had once spoken with a quietly assured but also a frightening sincerity to tell him that drowning was a very peaceful way to die. Eddie. That was it. The name was Eddie.

They were kids and it was summer, which meant long lazy and often aimless days in Saint Anne's Park in Dublin and even longer ones frittered away, as only youth can, roaming Bull Island. On this particular day, they'd left the park behind to use the old wooden bridge connecting Dollymount and Clontarf to the Royal Dublin Golf Links and the beach beyond.

It was just past the traffic bollards that they planned to swim under the watchful eye of Our Lady, Star of the Sea, as she offered protection to all who might need it from Dublin's North Wall. But Eddie never made it to the Bull that day. He was trying to catch a green backed crab when he slipped on the green algae of a small-boat slipway at Dollymount. Slipping from a slipway, good man Eddie.

Ignatius remembered watching for some time as Eddie simply looked back up at him from where he lay on his back, lying quietly amongst seaweed clumped rocks under less than two meters of water. He had no idea that Eddie was quietly drowning and at one stage, even waved down at him. The average age might have been anywhere between ten and thirteen, but it was hard to be precise with so many variables. For example, the 'gang' had no fixed membership, only ad-hoc and instantly forgettable rules and an extremely fluid leadership.

It was a federation made up of whoever was there on the day but luckily, one of them realised that Eddie might not have been totally happy with the idea of departing the world so young, and leaped in to his rescue. All hell broke loose trying to get them both back onto the slippery slipway, made even more treacherous by the volumes of ocean soaked up by their clothes.

It was unbelievable that Eddie couldn't swim, mainly because he came swimming so often. It transpired however, that his idea of swimming was just fooling around in shallower water. That was how he'd hidden his fear of deep water from everyone else and as a result, he never tried to conquer it or learn. But what was really shocking to Ignatius was how placidly Eddie accepted his fate. His fear was so great that once the water got him, he surrendered. Had he bothered to stand up and jump once or twice, his head would have broken the surface for air and Ignatius would have seen that he was in trouble.

Anyway, some weeks later, Eddie decided to share the details of his near death experience with a select few of those closest to him. The upshot was his quiet revelation that drowning would be his preferred way of dying, if he was ever offered a choice. He recalled Eddie once offering to lie under oath for his benefit, but apart from that, Ignatius couldn't remember him ever doing so.

So, two things struck Ignatius just then and the first was that Eddie was obviously right about drowning. The second was that it wasn't a requirement to be physically close to the statue of Regina Caeli in order to receive her protection. He thought it strange that Eddie turned out to be something of an atheist and just then, Ignatius decided he would look him up to hopefully pay him a visit quite soon. With that conscious decision made, the priest realised that he was still in that secure, happy and careless place maybe halfway between sleeping and waking or drowning.

Reality was still far away but his homecoming was timeless, until he shivered and other senses followed his reasoning. Cacophonous colourful energies came close to saturating his eardrums while his vision flooded with more flapping wings than he thought could be contained in just once slice of sky.

Gruff, cursing people enthusiastically added raised voices to the mix and something was whacked into the open palm of a painful right hand. He may subconsciously have abandoned the incident in the ether, but that impact brought install recall of a rabid penguin attempting to feed on his fingers.

He was cold and soaking wet but somehow alive, so he sat up to appreciate Skellig from the point of view of someone returned from the recently departed. The pristine spiritual oasis he'd left behind was replaced with absolute mayhem. At first sight, it was a rougher version of Skellig. This one was overrun with screeching chimpanzees wearing hairy human heads and wielding hatchets. A deep intake of breath brought more vital oxygen to his brain.

They were divided into two groups. A band of maybe twelve or thirteen were spaced along the biggest rocks of a shoreline bearing a superficial resemblance to that beyond the pebbled path area where he'd first come ashore. One of them stood close by and on closer inspection, he could see that he was just as wet as himself and wearing a malevolent scowl.

"NISH!" He screamed, pointing seawards.

A similar number of bedraggled made up a second group. These were in the act of clambering up the shoreline onto the rocks or engaged in hand to hand fighting with the first group who apparently had a problem with them doing so. He looked beyond the screaming and shouting to discover that the gurgling and sputtering ferry boats were nowhere to be seen.

They'd been replaced by six, no seven small black boats similar to the curraghs that were a common sight along the West Coast. The difference was that these might have been slightly longer, and with single masts and loosely furled sails in addition to wooden pegs for oarlocks.

The oarsmen and their 'passengers' were easily as ragged as those on shore and were attempting closer support for those engaged by the first group, who were intent on keeping everyone but themselves at sea. Ignatius stood up to get a closer look as well as his bearings, but he did so too quickly and got a throbbing headache instead. Eyes down and hands to temples, he saw the club lying on the ground at his feet. There was fresh blood on the narrow end that he guessed might have come from his own damaged fingers, and was just then on his face as well. He had the distinct impression that someone may have placed it alongside him for a purpose.

Those in the boats and yet to land, together with their colleagues climbing onshore could have potentially outnumbered the defenders by at least four to one. However, being already in possession of the higher if also the more slippery ground, that didn't look like it would happen too soon. There just wasn't enough places where the boats could safely disembark, and then he caught a glimpse of another boat directly below the rocks. So, that was where the front line of invaders were coming from, he noted with some satisfaction.

The boat people were being assaulted with everything from circular wicker shields, batons and clubs like one on the ground, though there was also more serious weaponry on display. He could see long-shafted spears and a plethora of hand axes. A stocky, barrel and bare chested individual was apparently content to use just his fists. Ignatius wiped his eyes again to be sure he wasn't still in dreamland.

A sickening dull thud followed by the splash of an inert chimpanzee thrown back into the waves close by, was confirmation that this was no mirage, nor a game being played. The attack and its repulse were matters of life and death.

The unfriendly wet ragamuffin turned away from him to take a swing at a rock crawler who'd made it as far as his feet. The fur-clad interloper was intent on literally cutting the same feet from under him with a long double edged sword, though he couldn't swing it properly. He could only use one hand while the other was stuck, limpet-like to the rock in an effort to keep himself from falling back onto those behind him, or the boat, or the sea. A glance to his left told Ignatius that the small quay was not where it should have been, but another thrown up behind him confirmed he was unmistakably on Skellig.

As long as the mysterious melee was in progress, he wouldn't be able to establish where on the island he was. It was obvious that he would have to get actively involved in his own defence or run away. He could just about remember his last fight, which was forced on him by an anonymous drunk in Dublin's Temple Bar. That place was always a magnet for troublemakers but thankfully, the guy was operating as a lone wolf. So once recovered from his surprise, he managed to send him packing for the price of a black eye and a bloody nose.

What he was looking at here was some kind of gang warfare and with real weapons. His inclination was to run, but to where? On top of that dilemma, he couldn't make heads nor tails of their language. Maybe, he thought, they were all foreigners or abandoned refugee immigrants or something.

Another deep breath and it came to him that he was a Jesuit, trained to soldier in the army of the Pope, the Church and Jesus, but a soldier nonetheless. That meant he had to recognise and accept situations where urgent action was needed. Maybe 'Nish' was a war cry, he thought.

"NISH". Ignatius shouted, coming to the belated realisation that he must have been rescued from the water by the nearest individual, who'd soon be outnumbered if help didn't arrive. Brother Chaz would be just the man for this he thought, and despite himself, he laughed out loud to suffer another withering glare from his lifeguard friend. This was just so insane.

Reaching gingerly down, so as not to antagonise his headache further, he retrieved the bloodied club and then looked around to see where help might come from. However, everyone in view was either facing Skellig from the sea or with their backs to it and already alongside him. Decision time had arrived and he applied the logic that any enemy of his friend must also be his enemy. An alternative alliance could well make an enemy of his friend, so he looked for a small patch of Skellig to defend from these wild men of the sea.

It takes an adrenaline fuelled mind to be ready for hand to hand combat and Ignatius wasn't quite there yet. He was carefully sauntering over the rocks to join his screaming lifeguard when a second heavily bearded invader rose slowly like a crab, from between the rocks to his right. This one was so intent on stealing in behind his chosen ally, that he only had eyes for his target. He hoisted a wicked looking long shafted hatchet loose from a belt around his waist.

Ignatius told himself once more that he was a man of god and sworn to peace, reconciliation and good will between all men and he was. However, it really didn't seem like he was going to be given the time to preach peace to anyone just then. So, despite the excruciating pain in his hand, he released his blood curdling scream. That was primarily to distract the assailant for a few critical moments, but also because it was what everyone else seemed to do as a prelude to a strike. Then he launched himself and surprisingly landed the club in a shocked face.

Teeth definitely and something else with more gristle than bone possibly, yielded to the blow which snapped the monkey's head backwards and upended his forward motion. With the fight taken out of him, the man melted back into the rocks. However, the stroke used to bring him down brought the club dangerously close to his ally's skull.

The Jesuit's new comrade in arms turned fearfully wide eyed at the sound of a whoosh so close to the back of his head, but then broke into a grin at the sight of animal skinned legs slithering off the rocks beside him, to then splash unseen into the sea below. However, the swinging of a club so close to a friend suggested a level of incompetence in the delicate art of murder, so he was directed to stand on the wet rock further away. They would do better side by side than with one swinging from behind the other.

"Fawlte rowat ahara." He said in a very sarcastic tone and the priest's ears picked up something familiar about the words, but there was no time to ponder them further just then.

"NISH." Screamed Ignatius, using a word that he assumed had something to do with action and pointed to the man with the precarious, one armed hold on the rock between his ally's feet. He'd managed to get a sword into his free hand and was about to try cutting his friend down to size once again.

There was no shortage of adrenalin there. A quick step back was followed by a high jump, which allowed the blade to swing harmlessly underneath. Then, like a man taking a short run-up to a penalty kick, his friend aimed a leather wrapped foot at the offender's head, where it landed squarely. It also carried enough force to throw the attacker from the rocks with a loud grunt and a retarded splash. Shortly afterwards, a man with a well bloodied nose was seen clasping his sword to his chest with two arms, like his life depended on it while kicking on his back towards a boat. He screamed an obvious obscenity and was then joined by others of his party, who had apparently decided to reorganise and select what they thought was a weaker spot to make a breakthrough.

With his sword handed to a colleague in the boat, the man swam back to help the one that Ignatius had clubbed. He seemed only semiconscious, but Ignatius was thankful he was alive though he didn't get to dwell on his victory.

A stealthy hand snaked up from a hole between the rocks to catch him around the ankle. And before he could react, his foot was whipped from under him. As he went down, a long spear came up from nowhere and at the blunt end of it was a wild looking red-haired savage with venom for blood and cold fire in his eyes. He'd allowed himself to focus only on the enemy he could see and didn't think of others climbing up through the rocks unseen.

This was a man who knew what close combat was all about, and with athletic agility and sureness of foot from years of practical experience, he was standing where Ignatius had stood just a moment before. Then he brought down the tip of his spear to hold it poised over the priest's pumping chest, while he clasped the shaft with both hands. From a viewpoint made possible from lying flat on his back, he could appreciate his opponent's far superior skill-sets. A hopeful glance towards his new friend offered no hope whatsoever, because he was also fighting for his life. It was a day for feeling doomed.

His conqueror, however had an opportunistic eye and paused when he spotted the thick links of silver chain that Ignatius wore around his neck. His anorak was already wide open and the spear tip was sharp enough to cut his soaked shirt, and then push the fabric out towards his shoulder. The chain was a gift from his mother, solid enough to hold the Jesuit Crucifix that Ignatius wore close to his heart. The spear-tip then scratched his heaving chest when it was used to lift the crucifix clear for a closer inspection.

Inexplicably, his 'would be' assassin, fell backwards into the sea by executing a reverse flip dive that wouldn't have been out of place at the Olympics. He then surfaced alongside his colleagues to await his turn at being helped back into their boat. Ignatius was instantly back on his feet and looking as intimidating as he dared, but failed when he almost slipped on the freshly washed rock.

He was caught between eternal gratitude for an obviously Divine intervention and the conundrum of what had caused it. He hefted the club onto his right shoulder and gripped the handle tight with both hands, while his knees shook like jelly.

The bout on the adjoining rock was also over when the sneak attacker was sent tumbling into the sea but at the cost of a wicker shield, which he refused to release. Turning his attention back to the boat, a discussion was taking place between a group of three or four thugs when the red face, red bearded man pointed Ignatius out.

"ARASH ANISH NAGURKIG - ARASH!" Came the shout from someone in one of the boats, though he couldn't see who. As it transpired, the shouted command was immediately complied with by both sides. Without pressing home any of some fairly obvious advantages, the defenders simply stepped just back from the conflict. This gave the invaders the time and space they needed to withdraw in safety and they accepted the offering. Ignatius was struck by that very civilised conclusion to a confrontation that was anything but mere moments beforehand.

His lifeguard might have been preoccupied with his own defence, but he wasn't oblivious to what happened on the rock next to him. He wore a frown over a puzzle and was obviously unhappy about something. His glare alternated between Ignatius and his flame-skinned slash red-haired adversary cum victor, now safely back on board the boat nearest to them.

With the flighting, shouting and screaming fizzling out, and the seagulls long gone from the murder and mayhem of crazed men, sound now carried easily between those on the rocks above and those inside the boats below.

"OWEN RUA?" It was a question directed by his new friend towards the man that had miraculously spared Ignatius, but he got no reply when Red Owen simply shrugged and sat with back against the small mast. However, the man next to him responded by pointing at Ignatius and shouting.

"DOOAH"

Ignatius didn't care what they were saying or what was going on. He felt that for a priest, he'd done his part in repelling the invaders and they could call him names all day long if they wanted to. But then, his own allies took up the chant while more and more of his enemies unmistakably pointed him out.

"DOOAH!" They shouted triumphantly and it was immediately joined by everyone else, except for the puzzled man next to him. They were reacting like he'd just won his bout instead losing it, only to be inexplicably pardoned. But he smiled back anyway, more out of relief than anything else. Maybe now someone would tell him what was going on.

"DOOAH!"

"DOOAH!"

"KAY HAY SHUH?" A voice from behind boomed power and authority, like someone back there had just come up with a megaphone.

"DOOAH!" Came the eventual shout from his saviour alongside and a giant of a man strode purposefully onto the rock beside Ignatius, who was lost in his shadow and also compelled by the sheer physical presence of the man into making more room. He moved too quickly however, and once again lost his footing to almost fall off shore to join the pirates, or whatever they were.

A massive hand caught him while he steadied himself and Ignatius found the time and space to look at someone who could have been cross bred between Conan the Barbarian and the Incredible Hulk but,

" - Dooah?" Was the only sound that came out of his mouth.

4 - SAME BUT DIFFERENT

It was only when the giant called 'Dooah' simply glowered imperiously down at the invaders, who were by then pulling back their boats, that Ignatius had time to focus on where he'd previously heard the words 'Fawlte rowat'. As it happened, it wasn't too far away. They are a Gaelic greeting for 'Hello' or 'Welcome'. However, the overly sarcastic seasoning with which his new friend had smeared them, would most likely be translated as 'About time'. All things considered, he couldn't have blamed him too much for the outburst.

That was the problem with Gaelic. It didn't need a huge dictionary because intonation was everything, and the pronunciation of any word could totally change its meaning. That was the main reason why Ignatius had given up on it at a very early age and how he found it easier to eventually swap it for another dead language, Latin.

Yet here he was, listening to the same language not just revived but replacing all others to become the vernacular in this isolated rural community. That was the only possible conclusion he could come to, until he took a closer look at the savages. They displayed a level of disregard for grievous bodily harm that he might expect from a people reduced to life in a post apocalyptic wilderness. That and the fact that they hadn't as much as a mobile phone between them meant something truly weird was going on. Worst of all, no-one spoke english, so it wasn't something he could discuss with anyone.

A humid breeze sighed through the rocks beside him and tried to whisper in his ear, but the pain in his hand was such that he couldn't listen. It was the kind of warm throbbing that comes with serious infection taking hold, and treatment was looking like it could be a world away.

After such a furious awakening from a sleep so deep that it may well have been death for a while, Ignatius suddenly had all the time he needed to unravel the conundrum of his dilemma. He began as he was trained to begin and identified the only certainty.

Descartes came to his rescue by reminding him that he could think and therefore he was alive, even though he'd come so close to death. It is also clear to him that death comes to everything one day, but what about near death? That was something that could arrive and be suffered on any number of days. He judged that despite the obvious difference in outcomes, death and near death were probably no different in terms of the anguish carried. Almost dying might in some cases be worse, because it brought no release from life and a future death waited.

He'd fallen about fifty meters into the Atlantic Ocean, barely missing any number of rocks en-route and had somehow survived. Some surreal encounter with a pissed off penguin caused him to stay underwater too long to make it back up to the surface in what remained of the same breath. His oxygen starved brain blacked out and just surrendered to drowning. Now he had that in common with Eddie but just like Eddie, he lived.

Then there was the impromptu hand to hand combat with lives at stake, but he didn't do that very well and lost, but yet lived. The mathematical likelihood of him actually dying that day, after the distress of so much near death, had to be negligible. If he wasn't under armed guard in some primitive jail, he would have seriously considered himself immortal.

Next on the agenda was the issue of the fickle nature of friendship and his new friend wasn't, simple as that. There was no doubt that the beast of a man they called Dooah was in charge, but it wasn't the giant who had clapped him in irons, so to speak. After a brief exchange of words with his dodgy friend, Dooah had disappeared just as quickly as he'd arrived. He couldn't know what they said, just as he couldn't tell them that tying his hands behind his back was as unnecessary as it was uncomfortable. After all, there was a guard with a spear, a hand axe, a long knife and a very short temper at his door.

There was no shortage of points to ponder, but the most pressing was probably Skellig itself. Brother Chaz would be the expert of course, but Ignatius knew there were more than three and a half beehive dwellings in the monastery area. He was sitting in one that was only about half the size of the others, but he knew there shouldn't be one this small. There was also supposed to be a church, plus an oratory somewhere and a series of terraces built into the southern peak, but there was just a very bleak park. There was no sign of the small pier and as far as he could make out, there was only one access to the intermediate saddle level between the peaks. He knew there would have been others though he wasn't sure how many.

The access they used was also incomplete with only intermittent steps that required him to be almost hauled up with a rope to stop him sliding back down again. Without that rope, it would be extremely dangerous to get up or down and especially after rain. And god knows that it always rains in Kerry.

The place was unmistakably Skellig but only because the main features were there, minus maybe the lighthouses. He wasn't too sure about them but hadn't seen them after his unexpected swim. He snorted and then realised that he could still feel the magnetic power of that unworldly presence, which may have grown if anything. He'd also seen Kerry in the distance as they climbed, or rather as he was hauled upslope regardless of vertigo. What was also noticeable about that was how empty the sea was with not one fishing trawler, coaster or lobster boat nosing around. There were only the shrinking black smudges of the dozen or so curraghs taking the wild men back to Kerry, though on a more southerly route possibly to Waterville. And yet, so much of the Skellig he'd learned about was missing.

"Domine propitius." Two silhouettes against the outside light. One tall while the other was slender, like a woman but both dressed from head to foot in robes, like classic aristocracy. These people were quite obviously a cut above the smelly animal skinned and mostly bare-foot savages overrunning Skellig that day.

"Huh?" Ignatius squinted towards what could one day become a door, but was just then a hole in a rock wall. The scruffy looking guard had taken up a central position so he could watch the proceedings. Then a third man appeared and the guard moved aside with a nod to let him pass. This one was slightly taller again and there was also something familiar about him. When he pulled down the hood of his robe while still outside, Ignatius recognised the friend who'd invited him to fight and then taken him captive for doing precisely that.

The taller of the two in front moved into the darkness and brought his bright white smile. He reached out for the silver chain and then yanked the crucifix free of his shirt.

"Quis es?" He asked politely.

He was speaking Latin. Ignatius sat bolt upright to get a better look at the man.

"Huh?"

"Quis es?"

"Oh. Yes … of course," he stammered and followed that with, " - Ignatius is anum dum." The thing was, he'd completely lost track of time except for having spent maybe the first hour of his incarceration resurrecting what he could of his junior school Gaelic. He realised his mistake when the silence refused to leave and they both looked to the third person filling the doorway cavity.

"Ignatius nomen meum." He had to be the best Latin speaker in college, but it still took time and effort to make the switch. The last thing he could have anticipated over sausage and scrambled egg breakfast, was begging his gaoler on Skellig for his next meal in Latin.

"Ah." The smile returned to his genteel interrogator.

"Erudimini." It was not a question, but he nodded to the suggestion that he might be an educated man. He felt his Latin bubbling up at the prospect of at last getting some answers to his questions.

"And you received that schooling in Rome?" He was polite but persistent.

"Rome yes … but also Dublin and Paris." The questioner lost his smile for the second time and again glanced backwards at the man blocking the light.

"France, for God's sake." Ignatius blabbered in english.

"You studied with the Franks? How is that possible?" Then man continued in latin, having extracted just one almost recognisable word from his outburst.

He then went on to elaborate "I am not ignorant like those who brought you here and I know something of metallurgy. I know that your crucifix was not crafted by the Franks, nor was it made in Soissons or Armorica so tell me, who was the bishop that placed it around your neck?" His inquisitor was becoming positively hostile and Ignatius scrambled for something that might remove an obvious misunderstanding. His Latin was flooding back so strongly that he was already beginning to think in the language.

"It was the Pope himself as bishop of Rome who honoured me with it and as a Jesuit, I have given myself in service to Christianity as a soldier." The Pope didn't personally confer his holy orders, but a white lie that mentioned the commander-in-chief in person seemed appropriate.

"Simplicius sent you to join Patricius?" He seemed shocked and surprised in equal measure.

In the gloom of his tiny prison, made even darker by the chain of interrogators blocking what little light there was, Ignatius caught sight of a simple wooden cross being nervously turned one way and then the other in the hand of the man facing him. Since they also spoke Latin, they were obviously members of some weird Christian cult, yet they didn't know the Pope. He couldn't remember precise dates, but he'd read somewhere that Simplicius was a fairly conservative Pope from way back, maybe around the end of the Roman Empire. That would have been the same period that Christianity was introduced to Ireland by Saint Patrick or Patricius?

"Wow." Exclaimed Ignatius.

"Wow." Mimicked the polite man who didn't hold back when he struck him with a closed fist. A girl shrieked and the man at the door rushed inside to stop the attacker pummelling Ignatius. His soft priestly face was beginning to look more like that of the losing boxer in the last round. Once restrained, the robed man with the wooden crucifix fell down at his feet.

"Forgive me." He was crying.

The woman was shaking like a leaf as she helped the confused man to his feet and both stumbled toward the door. As soon as they were out, the guard switched places. "Anish?" That word again.

Through an eye fast narrowing from at least one direct hit, he saw his friend cum gaoler slowly shake his head. "Nees Dayney." He muttered and then followed the other two out.

As it transpired, Ignatius had used his first hour more constructively than he initially thought. He was able to remember that 'Anish' was not 'Action' but 'Now', and

'Dayney' meant 'Later'. Something had just been commuted until later and all things considered, that had to be a good thing.

Then he remembered another useful word of Gaelic and shouted towards the guard. "Ishke" He couldn't remember ever being so sore but that wouldn't kill him. What he really needed was water.

The guard glared at him for some moments and then spat in his direction.

5 - DEATH AT LAST

Life to Ignatius was the accumulated memories of increasingly disconnected incarnations up until the total separation of the last one from all others. From the viewpoint of an out of body experience, he would have considered his own transition from childhood into the pubescent Ignatius individual and then into a student as a series of fairly smooth graduations. It was only when he became a priest that the really big issues arose.

He was a Jesuit for two brief periods separated by the devastation visited upon his family, and the original priest was irreconcilable with its more recent manifestation. However, the life he'd quite literally plunged into was easily as different again, and he found himself entertaining the notion of being an alien inside his own body. Unless of course, his body really belonged to someone else and he wished he could see if his hands really were his own.

He leaned his head against the wall to think and found some relief in the cool touch of stone on his aching head. After a while, however he found that lucid time spent thinking was merging into time spent dozing and daydreaming. In one of these, he smelled an Irish sausage and actually tasted cold spring water. Then he got a whiff of salted pork but his cold and by then numb fingers, distracted him from tasting either.

"Ishke." He'd shout periodically for water, but the guard continued to ignore him.

Reflecting further, Ignatius chose to deliberately disregard what was obviously impossible, and that was time travel. That was simply because it opened the door to inadvertently altering destinies in an already established present. Even the minutest change to yesterday could conceivably eliminate the only tangible reality, which is always today.

However, a quote from Arthur Conan Doyle reminded him that once he'd eliminated the impossible, whatever remains, no matter how improbable, just had to be the truth. He tried to apply that to the situation but discovered that he was no Sherlock Holmes and eliminating the impossible was actually his biggest problem.

That left two choices. Either he'd somehow fallen into a parallel reality in a time zone maybe sixteen hundred years behind local time, or he was drugged. The fact that he was so sore that he wished he was drugged, excluded the latter and so he was back where he started.

"Ishke." He called again but without expecting any response. The incoming light was also quite painful to his eyes, so he didn't bother to open them. Despite the fact that parallel realities were not just theoretical but also totally illogical, any parallel existence would have to deviate from the only reality that was apparent at the time, and that meant today. An alternate reality running in the past was just as ridiculous as time travel and yet the few names he'd so far heard were historically valid.

He dozed again and while doing so, realised that there could be a third possibility. That was the one in which he was already dead and awaiting final judgement. The idea came to him like the apparition that had quietly taken human shape before him, and then folded her wings with a soft rustle. She was a lot darker than the average angel, which set him thinking about dark angels. Maybe there was a prayer he should be saying to save himself from temptation.

Temptation? If time travel and alternate realities were illogical, then how plausible was yielding to carnal temptation with butchered hands still tied behind his back, and his tongue stuck to the roof of his mouth through thirst? There was also the inconvenience of eyes made mere creases in his punch drunk face. He thought that was a good joke and laughed. He was then rewarded with the sensation of a cool towel on his feverish brow and he wondered if angels might be somehow real.

Like scrambling upwards for air in Seal's Cove and then finding none, he knew that his body had to have slowed down for two reasons. The first was to conserve whatever critical air reserves remained and the second was because God is merciful and must sometimes show that by putting desperate people to sleep gently and with dignity. Then again, it could be that the first and the second reasons might in reality, be the first.

The angel put something in his mouth and he didn't struggle because he never feared angels, dark ones included. In fact, he had to relax further to hear her sing almost too softly. It wasn't Gaelic, nor Latin or English but it was a beautiful lilt in a style known as 'Sean Nos' by the Irish 'Traditional Music' fraternity.

Ignatius never did find the required enthusiasm necessary to master the Gaelic Language, but Irish music was in his blood. In one of those useless conversations you sometimes have with yourself, he'd come up with his own definition of 'Sean Nos'. He recalled going on record as saying it was a stringed instrumental in which all but the vocal chords are muted, and that sweet angel's voice took him straight to heaven.

6 - MAGUS

She was a vision that grew steadily stronger each time he was called out of his stupor, like a spectre sensing the presence of another. But she only spoke one word to suggest she might be real and that was a place that was also a name. So when his time came to withdraw into his healing place once more, he was compelled to consider how someone as obviously dark as Tara could had come to claim that name.

It also served as a reminder that the curse of rampant globalism could sometimes bring small blessings. After all, that was how exotic foreigners mixed with normal people to enrich genetic diversity and create new 'normals', but because her visits could be as brief as his own, he was still inclined to dismiss her as an illusion. There was however, the question of a fragrance that lingered longer than it should behind her, so he sometimes smiled in his empty room.

Tara administered potions, lotions, herbs and food that could be difficult to keep down. Most of the ingredients were both simple and familiar but others left the kind of medicinal tangs that robbed everything else of flavour. They did however combine to work like magic. She possessed a confidence in her ability that seemed to will his tortured hand into dexterity and also coax a closed eye open while making it impossible for him to refuse her ladled offerings.

Afterwards, she would disappear as quietly as she came, though her visits weren't totally silent. It may have been part of her practise to sing a wordless song of such subtle versatility, that it could send him back to sleep just as easily as it prised him out of it, which he preferred. But when every feverish dream ended by waking to that smile, then drifting away from her was no torture. In his muddled state, he sometimes wondered if she might be dumb and maybe he'd just dreamed that most unlikely name. But deep inside himself, Ignatius knew there could be problems looming when he found her wandering inside as well as outside those dreams.

God works in mysterious ways and an athletic young man, also in elegant robes, would sometimes show himself like a silhouette framed in the door of the small beehive hut, more of a cell really. All shadows are dark but there was more than a suggestion that he was at least as dark as Tara. He was like her in other ways as well and even more silent than the girl. Ignatius was positive they'd made eye contact more than once, but the young man never acknowledged it and tended to disappear as often as the mysterious nurse.

That occasional presence made Ignatius realise that whatever else might be going on, he was still a priest and that beautiful angels were bad news. As his fever and infection fell, it came to him as no surprise that such a beautiful and exotic girl was bound to have a guardian of her own. Ignatius was soon well enough to be ashamed of his thoughts and prayed to god for forgiveness, for answers and as normal for any Jesuit, for new opportunities to serve.

There is an undeniable duality to everything, even if they are often perceived as opposites. The northern and southern auroras are where solar, cosmic and universal energies are caught in gravity's net and then guided by Earth's electro-magnetic fields to flow through her. Once inside, they mix with latent Gaian forces that have only recently begun to tease our still primitive understanding. However, every container eventually fills and the product of that metaphysical catalysis oozes through Earth's porous crust at places like Skellig, in a placid ethereal flow.

Suspended somewhere between heaven and earth, Skellig's spirit lectured the priest in whispers through craggy cracks and the waxing and waning of waves far below, as tides rose and fell to the moon and the stars. Detailed disclosures sometimes delivered in words as countless as hail-stones were emphasised with others as heavy as peals of thunder, but also in the soothing susurration of rain brushing stone. Shrill assertions came and went in screeches like a gull's, but Skellig could also accede with enviable grace. Sometimes softly, like spray on the wind but additionally, with the luminous dangling of pitter patter drops enclosing crystal figments of worlds upside down, like rewards for more difficult discernments.

Like random metallic filings falling into place on glass above a magnet, Skellig refreshed a pattern that was first imprinted on his primal brain in an age long gone. No dreams disturbed Ignatius on the fifth night when his neurone energies found internal equilibrium and limbic resonance found harmony in the universal song of life.

7 - LUMINE DIEI NOVUM (New Light)

With dawn daubing the black stones grey around him, Ignatius conducted his daily Jesuit Examen from the corner of his beehive cell and from behind closed eyelids.

"There's been a change." He remembered his father's young nurse whispering conspiratorially to him that morning when he closed the door ever so quietly behind himself. It was the inimitable Irish way of telling him that his father had crossed an undefinable milestone on his pilgrimage towards death and he tried to pray for his resurrection.

Grief stricken was an unfortunate condition that many of us will see in others and that we hope none will ever see in us. But he could only surmise that his father's grief for his eldest son was such that he no longer had any reason to live and three things struck Ignatius about that.

The first thing was the state of his parent's marriage. His mother had to be equally grief stricken, but she was very much alive and if his father didn't think she was worth living for, then their marriage was not what it seemed. That came as a huge shock. Next was the collaboration of everyone in his father's assisted suicide. The whispering nurse with the quiet rustle of her uniform, much like that of his own priest's cossack, suggested that his father shouldn't be distracted from total immersion in his own demise.

It also suggested that medical personnel were party to the 'arrangement' and he wondered just when the practice of euthanasia had become legal. It also raised the irksome question of who was tasked with deciding when complicity with assisted suicide overrode the priority of saving the same life. If DNR, or do not resuscitate was policy, then where was it written and by whom?

It didn't seem like a good idea to stamp his steel-heeled, leather-soled shoes on the tiled floor or scream like a spoiled child in a room that was already as still as a crypt, so he just went along with the show. The third thing was the nature of the change that was witnessed by the night nurse and he tried to visualise it in reverse, because as far as he was concerned, he'd just then come back from the same approximate place.

His bed was a slab of thickly quarried slate, but it was covered with layers of thick grass turned into hay and topped off with one warm animal skin stitched roughly to another and then folded around him. He'd slept like the dead and awoke with no shoes. In a manner of speaking, he'd been abducted from his previous life but was delivered back as something that certainly felt more capable and useful, he hoped. He was whole in every sense and feeling every bit as immortal as he'd considered himself to be some days beforehand.

Ignatius was able to appreciate the totally illogical loss of his life and subsequent rebirth in revised form as analogous to his conscious dismissal of god and then god's inevitable return to him. He reckoned that the least he could do was accept his new life in exchange for the old and then go about using it for the benefit of 'all' according to his own priestly plan 'A'. There just had to be a purpose to everything and in that purpose he knew he'd find opportunities to make amends to god for his loss of faith. He was more than just ready and his highly mobile lips evidenced a fervent renewal of his Jesuit vows.

He was feeling so good that he wouldn't have been too surprised to see static crackle from his fingertips, like some biological diode. His eyes dared him to open them so he could leap up and rush through the door to meet whatever that new dawn might bring, but caution urged patience. He was, after all, still a prisoner though no longer restrained or beaten into needing a beautiful doctor. He caught himself smiling like a madman which only made his smile bigger because like a madman, he couldn't care less about the past having already decided that life had just begun.

A ragamuffin of a boy appeared at the door and offered him breakfast with a shout. The dark aristocratic young man stood mute behind the boy, who dropped a wooden bowl at the end of the slab-bed and then pointed to the wooden latrine bucket in the corner. It seemed like a reasonable exchange and Ignatius almost floated over to seal the deal.

The obvious downside to his recovery or deliverance was that Tara stopped appearing. Even before it hit his tongue he could taste the seaweed in the stew, but with his nurse now gone, he could only discuss the strange flavours with the walls. Then again, discussions with people who spoke only in dreams or in smiles with their eyes, could hardly be considered two-way affairs. However, he was trained to be more than comfortable with his own company and since it seemed he wasn't going to be starved, he finished his food and decided to immerse himself in more spiritual reflection.

That activity pointed once again to his apparent immortality, but at some stage it struck him as odd that he hadn't actually seen the guard block the light for more than a day.

"ISHKE!" He called loudly. He wasn't as thirsty as he'd been when his genuine calls had gone unanswered, but he wasn't sure if he remembered the words for 'Hello' when they simply materialised in his brain.

"FAWLTE ROWAT!" He called loudly in Gaelic. It had become just too quiet outside. The perennial Skellig of 'bicker banter' in gull-speak was noticeably muted and it seemed like the ideal time to take a new look at his parallel reality.

He blinked in the sun, which was still low on the horizon and a chilled breeze blew the last of the cobwebs from his brain but along with his shoes, heels up against the outside wall of the cell, there was only empty silence. Two larger cells were almost joined to his, which seemed puny by comparison, but further along was the third and largest building. Smoke was rising from a low fire outside that one and a dark man rose to his feet and then tuned towards Ignatius. Ignatius continued to pull on his shoes but was puzzled about the loss of his socks. Who steals socks?

"Aqua." The young man had dark olive skin and features that were vaguely familiar. Ignatius recognised him as possibly Tara's sibling.

"Gratias tibi." Ignatius thanked him in latin and took a small, crude looking ceramic jug and then a swig. He placed the jug on the ground and stood to greet the man, who was just a tad shorter than himself.

"Frater Tara est?" He asked.

"Satyan." He held out his hand and Ignatius took it, aware of the need for a solid grip to project a positive impression, even if it wasn't his first.

"Ignatius." He smiled brightly, guiding the young man to his left and out of the sun so he could get a better look. He had the appearance of someone from the Middle East, or maybe the north side of the Persian Gulf.

8 - EACHTRANNACH (Foreigner)

Any meeting of complete strangers in even stranger lands is bound to make for a lengthy discourse and so it transpired. Satyan's latin was terrible but the priest's was good enough to mentally autocorrect mistakes. The Persian's mother tongue was Pahlavi, though he claimed to be multilingual and mentioned Parsi and Dari amongst others. He was the youngest son in a previously wealthy family with estates in the north of the Sassanid Persian Empire, which turned out to be an enlarged Iran.

To communicate with non Persians, and he'd apparently met quite a few on his travels, Satyan was obliged to pick up latin, the Esperanto of its day. However, he was still something of a novice and so, the conversation stopped and started more than it could ebb and flow.

Ignatius was extremely thorough in his Examen. He was like a reformatted computer disk ready to be written with new data. However, the routine acceptance of information that his old self would have rejected outright as impossible, was no easy task. But as a Jesuit teacher, he was also a consummate listener. At the end of the lesson in progress, he would find his new purpose and he would give it top priority until he found another, or until he was somehow delivered from this illogical reality. But as he listened, he learned that there was nothing alternate about their shared reality. It was recorded history, as far as he could tell.

Ignatius took extra care to suppress his anxieties and listened attentively to Satyan, who was quite dedicated to the task. It transpired that Skellig was no longer in Kerry, it was in the kingdom of Iar Muhann or West Munster and Dooah, though he might look like Goliath, was actually king. Ignatius knew next to nothing about the history of the time and listened intently to his young lecturer who could have been no more than twenty-four or five.

Satyan claimed that he and his sister were all that remained of their immediate family after a countrywide famine coincided with a Hun invasion and a subsequent war with people he called Hephthalites. His choices were limited to gambling on the success of Emperor Peroz by joining him on a counter invasion, or the protection of his sister in the unfamiliar south of Persia.

He didn't say how or why he'd found himself in Ireland, and instead grew increasingly suspicious and secretive. When Ignatius gently prodded him for more information, while offering none about himself, the Persian eventually clammed up.

"Now you need to tell me where you came from, Ignatius and also what your business is on this rock in the middle of the ocean." Satyan was right to demand some answers. The long established protocols of travellers peacefully crossing paths depended on the free exchange of information.

"I'm from right there behind you," said pointing towards Dingle, "- and I came here by boat but then fell into the sea. From what little I remember of that, It would seem that I was saved by a man who would later throw me in jail." He laughed nervously.

"But you don't speak their language any more than I do, nor do you dress or fight anything like them. My sister says you have the hands of a scholar with muscles to match, all in your head. Further, your silver chain and crucifix as well as your shoes have aroused so much interest amongst these people you would call your own, that I have to assume that you prefer to hide your true origins." Such straight talking seemed to end the temporary truce.

"I am afraid that there is no-one here who will believe me Satyan, but that doesn't mean I'm hiding something. The fact is, the truth scares me far more than you could ever appreciate. I have died at least four times in almost as many days, which make me reasonably sure that the next time could be for real." Silence fell as the fire crackled but in the background, the previously muted gulls seemed to be quickly finding their voices again.

"Do you know what that means?" Asked the younger man.

"You mean the gulls?"

"Yes."

“I don’t know.” And he certainly wasn’t hiding anything.

“It means that the birds who were disturbed by the fighting along the shoreline below us have now returned and from that, we know the fighting has stopped. But we don't yet know who won.” He smiled darkly.

“It was very noisy the other day, when I was down there fighting with them. How come we didn’t hear anything like that?” He well remembered that no-one held back and that shouting and screaming was part and parcel of the conflict.

“We are sitting close to the top of this rock and sound from below is thrown outwards. You can hear some of it, but you must focus. My sister is always the first to hear it.”

“So, maybe she can tell us who won?”

“We will know when we live or die,” he answered simply, adding “- and that will be decided by whoever comes up here for dinner.” He laughed at his own joke.

“That must be why they left no guard at my door. It must be bad if they couldn’t afford to leave one guard behind.” He looked to the stone wall to his right remembering that he’d been dragged into the compound from that direction.

“I think you flatter yourself Ignatius. Where is your weapon and how many battles have you fought, not including your minor skirmish on the rocks below?” Satyan asked nonchalantly.

“So what do we do now?” His attempt at further fact finding had ended earlier than anticipated.

“Danel is also one of us … foreigners, but he is a real fighter. So he has joined Dooah and now lives or dies below. That just leaves Yoan the Gaul, who was injured in a similar encounter some days ago and who is now recovering in the cell next to this one, but he will still join us shortly.” The dark man rose and somewhat ceremoniously pulled his cloak from his shoulders to slowly draw a finely crafted sword from a scabbard at his side.

“That just leaves the women. Tara, you’ve already met but Oinah and Zabrine you haven’t. Our job right now is to protect them until the last, and I mean the last. Can you do that for my sister in exchange for nursing you back from an early grave?” He inspected both sides of his blade and then nodded to himself in satisfaction. Just then a heavily bearded and rather thick-set man with an arm in a make-shift sling stumbled out from the same beehive in which the ‘Gaul’ was reportedly recovering. So, Ignatius figured this to be Yoan.

“Since you don’t have a weapon, which has to be a form of insanity these days, let me offer you a choice.” He took a few steps that took him to the corner of the building, where he continued like a car salesman.

“They say you got lucky swinging a club!” He pointed to some very crude weaponry lined up against the building’s stone sidewall. Ignatius saw a long chunk of wood that bore more than a passing resemblance to a baseball bat, except for the evil looking shard of pointed metal that ran all the way through it. The roughly hewn nail then extended far enough to do some serious damage to whatever might stop it. Next to that were a couple of axes, one long handled and the other more wieldy. Hung on the wall was an assortment of small circular shields, all wicker.

"Where are the women?"Asked Ignatius, puzzled that he hadn't seen any of them during his discussion.

"They are gathered together inside and they've been praying and meditating towards god for our protection." He placed a hand on the wall.

"However," he went on quickly, "- because you like secrets, I will protect their door for as long as I can breathe. You and Yoan can meet the victors on the hill top just behind that low wall. If they are friendly, you can welcome them back but more importantly, help the injured. And if they are not," he shrugged, "- you will have the advantage of the high ground." Subject closed, he reached over to select a shield.

Left for a moment with his thoughts and with the notable exception of Dooah, or rather King Dooah, most of the men he'd seen were slightly shorter. That said, they were also quite athletic looking and/or of more solid build than himself, but their shields looked just too flimsy to offer them any real protection.

Ignatius wasn't a fighter and felt he could serve the common cause better by reassuring his doctor and her company and maybe by doing what priests normally do. That would involve joining and possibly leading them in prayer, but Satyan didn't offer that option. Men fought then and it would appear that women would fight later, but only if they had to.

He moved in and took the club in his right hand and then the long handled axe in the left. Any weapon that could put another inch or two between himself and his unseen enemy was good. Alongside them, Yoan yawned like he'd seen it all before and then reached inside the stone doorway behind him. He whipped out a short sword of the type associated with Roman Legionnaires, except it looked too new. It had the appearance of something forged only days before, which made a mystery of its origin.

"With my good arm like this, I can't carry a shield and also kill Christians at the same time." Yoan declared loudly in latin, and then followed it with a burst of mad laughter. He obviously found the prospect of dying on Skellig hilarious, but Ignatius froze. Why were they about to kill or be killed by Christians?

9 - SCELEC TEARMANN

The priest swapping the club and axe from one hand to the other, only to change his mind and switch them back again seemed to be a source of great amusement to Yoan. The Gaul's unkempt head was reminiscent of an unmade bed after a night of excess or of prolonged nightmares. His long, dark hair was thickly matted and morphed into an extravagant red-hued beard about halfway towards his jawline.

A series of slow head shakes was evidence of that amusement and they were followed by two steps further forward to put a respectable distance between himself and a comrade in arms lacking conviction. Then he took another step forward, presumably to reduce the risk of being inadvertently struck from behind by friendly fire. Ignatius wondered if he'd been given some advice by a mutual Irish acquaintance, but he didn't really care. When push came to shove, he would just swing his weapons like crazy and hopefully inflict more damage than he'd likely receive in the process.

The breakfast boy was extremely light on his feet and propelled himself over the hill-crest like a hare ahead of the hounds.

“Kerakeen! Kerakeen!” He shouted as he sprinted past both of them without a glance to make a beeline for Satyan outside the largest stone hut.

Satyan held up four fingers as the boy vaulted the wall like a trained athlete and then came to a sliding stop, nodding all the while. “Shah! Shah!”.

“Gus Dooah?” Came the next inquiry and the boy broke into a huge smile, rattling off a lengthy tirade re-enforced by the digits of two hands thrust into Satyan’s face and with much mimicry of sword slashing, thrusting and simpler blows delivered with clenched fists.

Yoan smiled. “I can’t understand much of their language, but it seems that you can now stand easy, warrior.” Said with undeniable sarcasm but also with the friendly touch of a sword hilt on his shoulder.

“Here,” he continued, “- put your weapons under my good arm and then go down to meet them. From what the runner has said, it seems there may be four wounded men that will need your help to get up here for attention.” He smiled indulgently, like a man who’d seen it all too many times before. Close up and under all that hair, he didn’t look much more than thirty something at most.

It didn’t matter to Ignatius whether he laughed or he cried, both were inadequate expressions of his monumental relief and Yoan clearly saw it.

"Don't get too attached to life, my friend. We must expect to do this again and again, until one day we get a slightly different outcome but in the meantime, I will try to teach you something about self defence, if not attack." He finished solemnly.

It was almost dusk before Tara and Zabrine got a break from tending the wounded, whom they placed in the small cell that Ignatius had used and the bigger one next to it. They had a willing assistant in the young girl called Oinah, who couldn't have been much more than fourteen or fifteen. It seemed like she was also no stranger to the ongoing conflict by requiring minimal instructions from the two more experienced women.

Some of the wounds inflicted brought Ignatius close to gagging. He got through it by focussing more on the task of taking as much weight as he possibly could from each injured man. Four were quite seriously wounded but they were not the only casualties. Other men were limping and also glad to get the help of his shoulder. However, no friendlies had died, though he would later be told that there was still time.

Meanwhile, he opted to stay out of the way, periodically running and fetching when he noticed anyone being overtasked. He ended up filling and then refilling clay pots with water from a shallow stone well as required. Breakfast boy was joined by another urchin and then a woman who both seemed to materialise from nowhere. They stoked up the fire, chopped up vegetables and diced what looked like meat strips to begin preparing communal food.

Dooah was last to return with a small entourage, though everyone was small compared to him. On one side was the man who'd locked him up and on the other, was Danel, who'd physically assaulted him. Seeing two obvious enemies so close to the king wasn't a good sign, so Ignatius tried to melt into the background. He sat on the perimeter wall to watch them for a while, though everyone appeared to be in reasonable spirits.

Ignatius had a good opportunity to re-appraise Dooah, whom he'd first assumed to be little more than an outsized and possibly simple 'grunt'. He didn't dress or look anything like royalty and it wasn't just the absence of a crown. However, he did have a way of carrying himself and his words carried better, even when softly spoken and it wasn't just a question of volume. People jumped when he spoke and ran where he pointed and everyone laughed when he did, otherwise they remained quietly attentive when around him.

Dooah sat on a voluminous wicker chair that creaked repeatedly under his bulk. It must have been kept in one of the beehive buildings and the king used it like a throne. His people gathered around him at his feet and though the priest did catch his eye once or twice, they didn't rest long. The king's quickly moved on to someone or something else and so, Ignatius found himself waiting, just like any other subject.

As dusk deepened further and the ochre sky took on darker tones of bloody orange, murmurs rose into laughs and cries as accounts of the day were recalled. Such casual normality mocked the fact of such a vicious battle survived. It was like conflict was being willed to sink with the sun and to simply be gone. An almost carnival atmosphere grew with the encouragement of the soft autumn breeze blowing over Skellig from the South to guarantee a mild night, despite clear skies.

There wasn't a tree on Skellig but little by little, a significant bonfire was being built in the centre of the compound. Firewood that had to be brought by boat from Kerry, or as he reminded himself, from Iar-Muhann would also explain the still arriving people. Some also carried jute bags of fruit and other food including haunches of pre-cooked and smoked meat. It soon suggested a full blown party, that had to be planned in advance and to the smallest detail.

The sky was soon dark enough to admit the brighter twinkling of larger or closer stars and the steadier lamp of a planet or two. They had to be Jupiter or Saturn he guessed but hot on their heels came the bar of the milky way galaxy. Her entrance was quite subtle but in next to no time, the sky was spattered with sparkling diamonds. He was still looking up when the crystal and velvet veneer was sliced through by a glowing meteor towing a flurry of smaller shooting stars behind it.

With his night vision so acutely tuned, it was a hugely spectacular if silent display, though he was getting a sore neck from staring up. He was rewarded when his irises expanded further to admit the full vastness of it and he noticed it slowly rotate. Ultra hi-definition compensated for super slow motion when the entire vista began a slow somersault towards dawn.

He was far away in every sense of the word when Dooah decided it was time to exchange words. Ignatius insulted everyone it seemed, when he didn't respond by hauling his gaze immediately back to Earth. The king had apparently done enough shouting that day and he was clearly unhappy at having to repeat himself.

"HUC VENI IGNATIUS!"

The priest's head turned so fast that he felt something in his stiff neck creak, but that combination of displeasure and authority had him on his feet faster than he realised that Dooah also had a fair command of latin. He needed an appropriate reply, though chanting the king's name just as his men had done on the rocks some days before, didn't seem to be appropriate somehow.

"Domine mi." He said, when he considered himself close enough. His latin would be lost on most of the ragged assembly, but Ignatius hoped that Dooah would accept his implied apology. The somewhat disconcerting hush promised to mellow when Dooah's scowl lost some of its darkness.

In a voice loud enough to demand silence from those still whispering, the king recited a short piece of Gaelic prose, but Ignatius could only understand one word and that was 'latin'. It was followed immediately by an exaggerated spit intimating a bad taste being left in the royal mouth and it struck a general chord. Whoops of laughter quickly revived the previously convivial atmosphere. His Majesty had apparently excused himself for speaking in latin.

"I would prefer to be a simple man amongst simple people Ignatius, but I was born to be king. That means that in addition to many other unpleasantries, I was also required to learn latin but to be honest, I don't like it because it carries lies too easily. It is a deceitful language but also the tongue of the wider world beyond ours and we need trade. We are also obliged to occasionally discuss issues of mutual interest with our neighbours overseas, so we all learn one other language."

He paused to overplay the ceremonial acceptance of a wooden cup offered by an attendant, who then filled it to the brim from an oversized pottery piece, while miraculously managing not to spill a drop. Dooah made a great show of ensuring that none of it was lost and then sniffed it like a fussy wine taster. But the similarity ended when he abruptly knocked the contents back with a loud gulp and a grimace.

"Waaah! G'huntok!" He cried and an enthusiastic roar went up. The reason for the general fervour was made clear when he gestured to the jug holder to begin freely dispensing the potent brew. Dooah knew how to handle people and he let the small crowd have their raucous way for a full five minutes. Then he raised his hand to restore a semblance of silence and he turned his undivided attention to Ignatius.

"It is with pleasure that I introduce Suivne, son of Aengus Mac Nadfri, the Christian king of Cashel who is my … no, our sworn enemy and also enemy to all our people and to our gods." Ignatius recognised the man standing next to Dooah as his lifeguard cum jailer, but he looked a very different man in his long hooded robe. He looked mysteriously druidic though it seemed he wasn't overly eager to speak, so they just exchanged polite nods.

Even though seated, Dooah was tall enough not to be obliged to reach up to place a comradely hand on Suivne's shoulder. He simply reached over and then dropped it. "Suivne professes himself to be a spiritual monk and that would normally make his parents proud of their righteous son, but this is a son who does not suffer fools. His British mother sold her Roman lies and god to his father but not to Suivne, who saw her deceit. He was forced out of his birthright and into exile, but he now stands next to me as my own son."

Talk of volatile affiliations brought it home to Ignatius that he was part of a small but functional court, temporarily removed by the necessity of war to the frontiers. It was certainly primitive, but he was looking at the representative elite of ancient Ireland, an island of forests, rivers and bogs with no centralised settlements. The entire population would have only been three hundred thousand at most. Such small numbers would make wars of skirmishes, but a king was still a king.

Suivne was noticeably less inclined to banter like he'd done when they first met. This reinforced the concept of a court with protocols to be observed. The celebratory atmosphere was probably just enough to take the edge off what was a formal event, so he decided to follow Suivne's lead by saying as little as possible. He would wait until he was asked a direct question before giving a reply to meanwhile soak up as much information as he could gather.

His silence was apparently expected and Dooah continued in the same, now not unfriendly tones. "You also speak latin, Ignatius. So I will leave it to you to introduce yourself to those who share this language because I don't care to speak it much longer. We people of Munster now have many obligations to observe in honour of the gods and also the bravery that we were fortunate to witness today, including that shown by our enemies. I have no intention of insulting any of them by speaking their names in latin simply for your convenience. I will use the language of this land to which you are an obvious foreigner." The pause seemed quite deliberate and maybe represented an opportunity for him to refute that observation, but since he knew nothing about his own arrival, he bit his tongue.

Opportunity lost, Dooah continued. "As such, you cannot leave this place without my knowledge and consent. I will not tolerate foreigners with hidden agendas wandering our lands." Ignatius got another chance to see how big the man was when he stood head and shoulders over everyone else to make his way towards him.

"Over the water lies Munster and the other seven kingdoms of Ierne, but I cannot welcome you there unless you accept two simple rules." A long right arm gestured east before going on.

"The first rule is that to walk alone in my kingdom, you must pledge your allegiance above all other allegiances to me. That will include all religious and divine allegiances. The second rule will prove the first by obliging you to do as I command, regardless of who might be offended. All of my people have placed that trust in me and there will be no exceptions."

He let that sink in while he dropped his left hand to accept a refill from the official dispenser of drinks. Dooah then raised his cup to everyone in an unidentifiable toast but drank only some of it. Towering over the priest, he then offered him the cup and Ignatius was perhaps too keen to accept it, because the king quite suddenly withdrew the offer.

The king leaned down to speak in more confidential tones. "I will give you time to think about your precarious situation Ignatius, but you should know that if you can't accept the law of my land, you may never leave Scelec Tearmann. Tearmann is a word from our language that we apply to this sacred rock on which we now stand. As you can see, it lies at the very edge of my Kingdom but is still very much within it and I have vowed that it always will. However, like my father and his father before and by royal decree, we share the jurisdiction of Tearmann with the supreme god who presides over it."

Dooah had a look of such intensity that Ignatius was reminded of a hunter in the final stages of stalking his prey. He seemed ready, even eager to strike a final blow. "I know every sacred stream, every holy well, hill, mountain and tree in my Kingdom, and I know Tearmann better than anyone alive or dead. This blessed rock speaks to me in a language older than latin and I suspect that you already know if you are welcome here or not. The fact that I've seen you attempt to defend it from defilement and that you still breathe before me, suggests that God approves of you being here but presume nothing from me. Tearmann has been known to lose undesirable people just as mysteriously as it seems to salvage them from the surrounding sea."

The king's head straightened to regain its previous, respectably regal distance. "I choose not to judge you until I know more about you but if you displease me, I will remove you from Tearmann's protection when I return to my kingdom after tomorrow's fast. That is not to say that you may then set foot in Munster."

The cup looked tiny in Dooah's huge hand but it was pressed with surprising gentleness, almost reluctance into it the priest's left hand. Then the big man gripped his right hand with his own and shook it with a firmness that suggested major restraint.

"I will summon you later tonight when we can speak with the Persian." He said.

His unease forced him to speak prematurely, because no question was asked.

"With Satyan?" He asked, recalling their undeclared animosity, wondering if he now had three enemies to contend with.

"No, not him, Ignatius. Magus Tara accepted my dominion when Tearmann first called her here. It was a puzzle to me that she chose to remain here amongst foreigners when she has earned the right to my fire and my protection, but maybe I'm beginning to understand that now.

Anyway, we are all grateful to her because she has saved many lives and also provides me with wise counsel. So, I plan to ask her what she knows about you and then you will tell me if what she says is true, so don't get too drunk this night." He paused before adding, "Slawnte."

Ignatius figured the best thing to do was to say nothing more. In an effort to satisfy local custom, he knocked his drink back just as Dooah had done. But when the high alcohol content scorched his throat, he knew that he wouldn't be able to speak anyway. The only positive aspect was when he remembered the appropriate Gaelic response.

"Slawnte Uasal." He replied, careful to avoid taking a breath that would draw the liquor's potent fumes into his lungs, which he knew from bitter experience, would result in a coughing fit.

Dooah winked with just a hint of a smile and then backed away to join more familiar faces.

10 - LUGHNASA

Skellig is the ultimate paradox of the immovable object in often harmonious conflict with irresistible forces. It embodies history as well as timelessness and majesty by divine design but also wild simplicity, and it humbles evolution's most ingenious creation so far. It is more than a rock semi-submerged in weather and the sea. It is the epitome of stoic perseverance with impossible aspiration.

Ignatius noted that anyone attempting to live in such splendid isolation would need to imitate Skellig to simply survive, and he saw many such people assembled that night. They were a hardy people still aloof from mainstream humanity and embryonic civilisation, but they were also grossly underestimated. They belonged to an older, tried and tested order that had long ago proved that basic or functional does not necessarily imply 'primitive'.

Another enthusiastic cheer greeted the lighting of the bonfire, which added much needed light, though at a cost. Spark swarms spiralling up and then away on the breeze dulled the pristine celestial tapestry to which they aspired, but there is always a time for change. The cold alien vastness of a galaxy daubed across the sky, yielded to something more intimately human in the warm rose and red glows of the fire and from the smiling faces gathered around it.

From his remote analytical perspective, he could see that no wooden cup could stay empty and that each required constant refilling. Once surrendered however, a cup would not be offered again. Supposedly primitive elders could argue quite angrily with each other, but younger people were expected to soften opposing stands with mutual concessions. Compliments were graciously received but required at least two by return and foreigners like himself were easily forgiven, though frowned upon if they made the same mistake twice. A good example was when he chose to retain his cup after draining it, thereby depriving someone else of its use.

Those tidbits were learned by simple observation and without him having to exchange a single word which, all things considered, was probably just as well. Just then, Ignatius had to add one more, in that supplying food at these gatherings seemed to come with the risk of getting none of it yourself. In worlds placed as far apart as it was possible to be, people long dead were resurrected and made incarnate for his own enlightenment.

Mindful of Dooah's caution to stay sober, he'd moved to the periphery of the gathering and leaned up against the stone wall, though this time facing east or north-east towards the mainland. Out there in the darkness, silently and as if in response to theirs, countless bonfires blossomed into existence to apparently compensate for the stars he could no longer see above. But he wasn't left alone with those thoughts for too long.

“Greetings, Ignatius.” Came a voice from an apparition behind him.

He turned with some surprise and then added caution when he recognised Suivne.

“Greetings to you, Suivne.”

Both of Suivne’s hands were covered by the long arms of a robe that was, on closer inspection, a lot tougher than it first appeared, like felt. Aware of his suspicions, Suivne slowly revealed his hands. One was empty and the other clutched a half filled cup, but palpable distrust suggested that any time spent on insincere platitudes would probably be time wasted.

So, Suivne came straight to the point. “Dooah was not pleased to learn that I had you confined up here, where you could do no mischief. It was he who ordered you placed in the care of the eastern healer, but you shouldn’t assume on such kindness. You see, I am not as superstitious as the king when it comes to Scelec Tearmann. He will soon depart and if I see you as a threat to anyone here, I won’t hesitate to have you dropped over a cliff and sent back where you came from.”

Such blatant hostility from someone who could fight as well as Suivne was a real problem. His presence was enough it seemed, to antagonise only the most educated of them, Dooah included. They were spoiling for a fight but he wasn’t stupid enough to think he could win, so Ignatius backed off a little to reflect on his situation.

"I am no danger to anyone here Suivne, except perhaps to myself."

"That Crucifix of Rome around your neck tells me otherwise, though you intrigue some of us by what you could hope to achieve here without Cashel. That is, unless you are a coward of an assassin sent to trick us into believing that you can't fight. Had I seen that cross in the water, I would have stood on your head and kicked you deeper." Suivne tapped the priest's chest precisely where the crucifix hung, under a shirt long overdue the laundry basket.

His Jesuit training covered everything including managing hostility. It was only logical that allowing it to build unchecked would guarantee some critical mass sooner, rather than later. However, as he mentally fine-tuned his tactics, he caught sight of Danel over Suivne's shoulder and his still blackened eye twitched in recognition.

Danel didn't seem too interested in their discussion until eye contact was established and then held. That done, he cut short his conversation with a short stocky man, who had the misfortune of a hunched back. It was dark but by the light of the fire, he could see Danel's grin turn to a sneer as he got closer. Ignatius wasn't a fighter but he would have to tackle the problem before it tackled him, again.

So he raised his voice to guarantee being overheard by more than just Suivne and Danel. "Yes, I am a man of god and yes, I have studied in Rome, but I have dedicated my life to the service of real people like these as much as I have to the Church. I can also say that in the short time I've been a priest, I've offended no-one but God himself."

He waited for Danel to join them before finishing. "And because god is merciful, I am not just forgiven but spiritually reconnected from this holy place." Not many of the common people would understand latin, but he said it loud enough to alert them to the probability of an argument. If he was going to disappear over a cliff, he wasn't going to make it easy by going quietly.

"So, you confess to being a priest?" Danel's ears were already tuned to the discussion.

Then he spat the word to make it an accusation. "A PRIEST!"

He reached over to grab Ignatius by the throat, but the Jesuit saw it coming and blocked it with the reaction of a raised forearm. Danel's hand disappeared under his robe to produce a small knife, though the blade looked long enough for its purpose.

"DANEL … NO!"

Suivne pushed himself between Danel and the priest and an anxious silence was permitted to tick impotently past.

"Dooah didn't punish you for beating him up earlier because you couldn't have known that the priest was under the protection of Tearmann. But he punished me by making me responsible for this priest's safety."

"Gaaah!" Danel's frustration boiled over and then fizzled out when he re-sheathed his knife, turning to count anxious faces behind him as he did so. Then he laughed loudly and said something in Gaelic, which they found amusing enough to quickly lose interest again.

Danel leaned close to Suivne. "King Dooah hasn't yet lost all of his family and friends to the Church of Rome and their evil alliances. Everyone who was important to me, everyone apart from my daughter, lies either buried in unmarked graves between Gasteiz, Suebi Gallaecia and Armorica. That or they've been enslaved or worse." He hissed malevolently and continued without blinking.

He spit out the words in a latin mantra, committed to memory possibly for the purpose of subsequent recall when courage in battle might need to be fortified by hate. "First by the Visigoth Euric and then by Burgundy into Soissons, before the unholy alliance of Euric and Rome took the last of them from my bloodied fingers. The old world may have cried during the fall of Rome, but I freely admit that I praised god for some semblance of justice." His hand was still on his knife while Ignatius searched for something to say.

"I know nothing of that." He said softly.

Danel still hadn't blinked. "How can you wear a Pope's cross and claim ignorance of the crimes committed in the name of Jesus? Tell me where you've been living before Tearmann took pity on you and if I know the name of that place, I will call you a liar." Suivne reached over and placed a comradely hand on Danel's shoulder.

The gesture seemed to carry considerable empathy with respect and had an immediate calming effect. Danel finished his monologue in softer tones. "There is no place-name written on any map, whose people are unaware of who is responsible for bringing these end times upon us."

So much animosity couldn't exist without a valid reason, but Ignatius was genuinely too ignorant to respond to the challenge. He couldn't tell them he was from Dublin, because it would be centuries before the capital city would become identifiable by name. Further, any mention of the Church and Rome only drove everyone on Skellig crazy. He was caught between the proverbial rock and a hard place, a priest who daren't tell the truth.

Danel hadn't tasted wine for far too long, but he wasn't keen on strong liquor or what passed locally for beer. Just then, he needed to quaff something and like a telepath, the steward cum waiter squeezed through the small group at the fringe of the gathering. Danel took a cup but became impatient when it wasn't immediately filled. Suivne then chastised the waiter with some harsh words of Gaelic, but from what Ignatius could gather of the exchange, their raised voices were causing the dispenser of drinks some concern. It seemed to him that he was also responsible for maintaining order and civility.

Snatching at the chance of killing two birds with one stone, Ignatius drained what was left of his cup and then extended it to the waiter in an effort to present a common front, one with no obvious acrimony. However, in his rush to milk the situation, he'd forgotten how strong the liquor was and his red faced grimace didn't look anything like the relaxed smile he intended. Then he made the mistake of taking a deep breath, which brought on the coughing fit he had time to anticipate earlier with Dooah, but it worked.

Not a drop was spilled, which was a vital point of etiquette and the waiter thought his contorted face hilarious. Despite himself, Suivne couldn't help but guffaw and even Danel's tight, grim face loosened a little. Apparently satisfied that decorum was restored, the waiter wandered away chuckling to himself.

"There are things that I simply can't say without making my situation worse." Said Ignatius, when he'd recovered enough to speak.

"You're a priest of Rome. There is nothing worse than that." Danel hissed, but frustrated by the impotence of unsatisfied rage, took a sip from his cup instead. His face reasonably mimicked Ignatius just moments before, and another dangerous moment passed when he got no pity and the three of them shared another light moment.

"Let me promise to explain everything in due course, but just not tonight." He was under no illusion that the subject could be revisited anytime. His only option was to push that inevitability further into the future and it was Suivne who was first to make a small nod of agreement.

"Tomorrow then." The druid slash monk was apparently more familiar with the potent brew and didn't even blink when he sampled his own.

"Tomorrow." Agreed Danel, eventually.

Suivne filled the silence that followed. "Are you familiar with the honouring of our old gods, like Lugh and his mother, Tailtiu the Earth Goddess?" He asked the question conversationally, but it was unclear whether he was addressing Ignatius or Danel.

"There are many in Gallaecia who still celebrate Lugh on this night, though they wouldn't dare trying to appease two gods in one celebration. That would invite divine discord and retribution but as a true Christian, I have left such superstitions behind me. What about you priest?" Danel opted to replace overt hostility with the option of flushing out some useful intelligence.

Ignatius could vaguely recall reading a story or maybe watching an old movie called 'Dancing at Lughnasa'. It was an old Celtic feast that occurred in late summer but because he knew dangerously little about the old gods, he would have to choose his words carefully.

"Where I came from, the old gods are mostly distant memories, but they are increasingly celebrated by people who call themselves 'New Age'." He paused and then mentally chastised himself when those two words raised eyebrows, but he pushed on by adding. "In fact, even the new god has lost much of his appeal, which is part of the reason I became a priest."

"What is the other part?" It was Suivne.

"A vocation, to serve people and God together and I would be lying if I didn't admit to some pressure from my family," another pause, "- especially my mother."

Suivne laughed aloud. "I can attest to the occasionally abusive power of mothers in pushing their sons away from the dangers of sword-play and into monasteries and holy books."

He touched the wood of his cup against the one Ignatius held in both hands and sipped again, obliging both the priest and the Gallaecian to join him. Danel was still curious, however.

"And how do you propose to serve both people and God together?"

Put on the spot and only too aware of how angry the word 'Rome' could make his already fiery opponent, Ignatius chose to make his answer vague and people oriented. "I teach mathematics, philosophy and morality and I am also sent into the world with others to help the poor to cultivate crops and to help them feed themselves."

"Why would farmers who are the acknowledged masters of crop cultivation need help from you, who has been trained in mathematics, philosophy and morality?" Danel was intrigued about priests digging fields for farmers and Ignatius couldn't really oblige him with answers.

Climate change with population explosions and pressure from commercial biofuel and other environmentally damaging crops like palm oil just wouldn't be appreciated in a world with a global population that could fit comfortably into a single twenty-first century city.

"Things are very different where I come from." It sounded trite but it was all he could say and Danel's face told him he wasn't happy with it.

"And in return for your education and tillage expertise, you impose the Roman god on them to spread heresy and chaos." He was furious but so was Ignatius. He'd been walking on eggshells all day and still knew nothing about these Christians who fought Christians. The reformation, Martin Luther and Calvin were more than a thousand years in the future. It was natural that they wanted to know more about him, but they were all walking enigmas.

“So, what about you Danel? What kind of Christian heretic kills other Christians?” He spat it out and the two of them glared at each other. Dark clouds that had shown signs of lifting dropped back to bring a deeper gloom.

One of Suivne’s eyebrows arched and his head went back as if seeing Ignatius in a different light. Then he dropped a hand on Danel’s shoulder to quietly ask him. “Could it be that he knows nothing about Priscillian, Instantius, Silvanus, Ithacus or Idacius or even our own Pelagius?”

It was like someone had struck Danel. He dropped his cup and its contents into the wiry grass and then placed a hand on each of the priest’s shoulders. “We have countless reasons to despise those who promise a new age, without suffering with real people to survive in what they have made of the old one. The time for either honesty or retribution has come on this auspicious night of Lugh and the truth of where you come from will longer wait until dawn.”

Ignatius would have to come clean and if they thought him mad enough to murder, then he would have to face that possibility if it came. However, being drunk on Lughnasa was tolerable and maybe desirable for some, but a drunken brawl on his feast day was more than just irreverent. Their raised voices together with the spilling of liquor, were once again attracting attention.

While the priest dithered over which of his many disasters could be the best place to begin, the young runner was as nimble in the dark as he'd been earlier that day, and also just as fresh. He burst through a group of stern, disapproving faces.

"An Ri." He announced and followed with a loud, "Anish," when no one immediately jumped in response.

Ignatius was puzzled.

"We've been summoned by King Dooah." Said Suivne, scowling at Danel.

11 - SEANNCHAI (Storytellers)

An old man with hair thin enough to be made of cobwebs sat on the left side of a stone slab big enough to cover any crypt. Dooah occupied most of the middle section, while the reason for the pleasant fragrance wafting through the stones of the largest beehive hut, sat regally on the king's left. Yoan and Satyan seemed very much at ease on the floor, with their backs against the wall. The Gaul gestured to the three of them to join them, but then glanced at the king and it was ominous that a royal nod of approval wasn't automatic.

The king posed Tara a wordless question and like him, she answered with a slow considered nod. When she needed to follow that up with a whisper in the royal ear, Satyan took it as a cue to do likewise and shared a quiet word with Yoan.

It was clear that one or possibly all three of them were the subjects of an earlier discussion. The king was not in a very good humour, but that was nothing new.

"You have eaten from Lord Lugh's table and drunk from his jug, but then bicker like bitches left tied up and starving to keep watch in the darkness." Dooah could have been heard in Ventry.

"Domine." Danel was on his feet but quickly learned that routine appeasement wasn't going to cut it this time.

"SILENCE WHILE I'M SPEAKING, FOREIGNER."

“Yes Sir.” A gesture from Dooah gave him permission to slink back onto the floor.

The king then swapped some informal exchanges in Gaelic with Suivne, who remained seated throughout but, who gestured between Ignatius and Danel in turn as he spoke. He was, no doubt, supplying some background to the argument that had so displeased a king and at least one god.

“Dyuk.” Dooah shouted to no-one in particular but mere moments later, the overworked jug bearer arrived in the empty doorway. Ignatius had had enough strong liquor and Danel had totally lost his taste for it. Satyan first and then his sister politely refused, which left the King, Yoan and the old man to raise a silent toast to each other and no doubt, Lord Lugh.

Dooah’s fickle nature surfaced again when he unexpectedly dropped the subject of the brawl right there. He was apparently required to admonish the perpetrators for their crude behaviour, but sentencing for the crime of divine displeasure was left to the discretion of the slighted god.

“This is my friend and wise counsel of long standing, Rudgael Dairinne. He is one of a chosen few, who is kin like me and through blood with the kings of Ailleach, Dal Riada, Connacht, Meath, Thomand, Oriel and Leinster. He understands latin but he can easily get embarrassed and so, won’t be speaking tonight.” Rudgael rose and offered a barely discernible bow and a smile severely short of teeth.

“We are people that Rome considers irreligious pagans, but tomorrow is the day of full fasting. As there is much to be thankful for and even more to contemplate. I will therefore spend this Aoine aloft and alone in meditation on Tearmann’s highest peak and as close as I can get in this life to Great Dagda. I urge any of you who claim godliness to take some time away from your cares and to join your prayers to mine. On the following day I must return to my Kingdom to prepare labour for the harvest and to recruit men for war with Cashel, Oengus and Eithne. They have solid allies in Leinster, Meath and also the mad bishop of Armagh and of Rome.” Dooah’s thick wicker throne creaked loudly as he leaned back into it.

Listening to him speak, it was understandable that Dooah didn’t like latin because he did seem to labour while expressing himself. Ignatius deduced that fatigue might have also made him irritable after a lengthy battle. He was also required to preside over subsequent rituals to satisfy multitudes of gods and men. The result was that his latin sounded worse than it normally did but with all that the day had thrown at him, not least copious quaffs of liquor and beer, he was still an imposing, if gruff presence.

It had to be close to midnight when his cup briefly touched his lips and he continued. “I have much to do to mend fences with our western and northern neighbours, but I must match Cashel’s alliances with my own in Thomond, Connacht and Aileach. That means that I won’t be returning to Scelec Tearmann until we are victorious. I will however, leave instructions for a boat with essential supplies for my two young grandsons, Owen and Dallan. I have asked them to make themselves available to you from time to time, but their principal duty is to report unusual boat movements and such like to me. Cashel and Oengus will most likely be just as busy as Munster and I doubt they will bother you, especially since they'll no longer see me as an easy target out here, far removed from my army." He laughed at that since Cashel's latest attempt to remove the king of Munster from his kingdom had cost them considerably more than they'd bargained for.

Dooah absentmindedly kneaded the sore knuckles of his right hand with the left, recalling perhaps a blow or two struck and then looked down more benignly on faces he probably wouldn't see again for some time. After sharing the fight and the festivities and then spitting out harsh words, he felt obliged to share his concerns.

"Then again, Cashel might decide to take Tearmann while it's not defended simply to goad me into spending time that I don't have in retaking it."

He continued shaking his head as he went on. "I no longer have a reliable spy in Cashel to tell me what Oengus is planning, but I also can't afford to leave able bodied men here to defend a non-strategic rock, however dearly I hold it. But I do implicitly believe that Tearmann protects what it considers worthwhile, just as it's been known to lose what it considers useless. All I can do is pray from the southern peak for the gods' protection to continue in my absence."

He raised his free hand above his head in a gesture to one or all of his gods. "I will be back on Tearmann to light the Imbolc bonfire and to dedicate our final victory to Dagda."

Suivne was smiling when he whispered to Ignatius. "Imbolc marks the beginning of spring, so it looks like being a long winter, unless you're ready to bend that holy knee to Dooah and ask him to take you with him to Munster."

The thought had certainly crossed his mind, but Ignatius couldn't be sure what terms and conditions might be applied to citizenship. The king pointed at Satyan.

"I've spoken enough accursed latin for one day while my storyteller makes Cuchullain even taller and faster with every word spoken to those around the bonfire, so you can take his place. After you, I will hear Danel. Yoan can tell me his story when we reach Ventry. He and Zabrine have sworn to serve me as king and I them by return. He has bought land in Munster and he will pay for it with his sword arm and his war experience. Magus Tara already enjoys the freedom of Munster, but she chooses to stay on Tearmann for now. So I will hear you last, Ignatius."

Satyan slowly rose to his feet but his eyes were fixed on his sister, as if waiting for a cue. When he said nothing, she spoke some words that sounded like Arabic but which Ignatius assumed to be old Farsi.

Her advice seemed to do the trick and Satyan began hesitantly. “My latin has been so poor King Dooah, that I begged forgiveness for speaking countless mistakes.” It took him some moments to get the gist of what the Persian was trying to say. Ignatius wondered if the young man would be capable of stringing more than a couple of words together, but he conscientiously persevered. Slowly but surely, his stuttering pauses and occasional lapses into Greek diminished, as did a prolific disregard of grammar as he gained confidence and no-one laughed to undermine him.

It was quickly made clear that Danel and Suivne were already familiar with Satyan’s story because they were quick to offer corrections or more appropriate latin words here and there. Even King Dooah helped the narration by clarifying some of the detail, particularly names and dates in a remarkable story of survival in an ancient and very hostile world.

Knowing he would soon be required to give a credible account of himself, the priest’s mind snatched at some half truths that might be built into something that wouldn’t get him locked away or beaten up again. However, the story of Satyan and his sister was so compelling that he unconsciously gave up on that exercise to listen. He’d just fallen off a cliff and then continued through time, but these two young Persians had crossed three empires and survived countless wars in the process. It also transpired through the telling of his story, that Satyan had something in common with both himself and Suivne.

All three were strongly encouraged by their respective families to enter religious life. He as a Catholic Jesuit, Suivne as a monk, and Satyan as a Zoroastrian priest. However, there the similarities ended because while Ignatius was raised in the relative austerity of middle class Dublin, Suivne and Satyan were born with silver spoons in their mouths. Suivne as the son of King Oengus of Cashel and Satyan, a distant relative to King Peroz of Persia, though not so distant that his family dynasty wasn't extremely wealthy.

The worlds in which Satyan and Tara were cast adrift must have seemed like the apostle John's end-times-revelations being enacted. Persia had just come through a particularly destructive civil war and King Peroz committed himself to rebuilding it. However, a famine lasting seven years put a stop to those efforts and also decimated the population, along with the Satyan and Tara family fortune.

The full extent of the drought was measured, according to him, by the unprecedented fact of both the Euphrates and the Tigris rivers running dry. His family survived, but a Barbarian invasion almost immediately afterwards coincided with Persia's on again off again war in Armenia. Ultimately, it was the White Huns who made them refugees, though they had no concept of how far they would travel in search of peace.

Satyan threw out names that meant little or nothing to Ignatius, but an alliance between Persia and a people he referred to as 'Hepthalites' stood out. That name had come up earlier in the day but Satyan's elaboration included an account of an alliance with them that went sour quite quickly. Apparently, Peroz cheated on an arrangement to include his sister in marriage as part of the deal, but delivered a servant instead and so, yet another civil war began.

What was left of the family were driven from their newly acquired lands and they fled further west into the Byzantine Empire. Satyan and his sister were little more than children and as such, they were permitted to settle in Greece for a number of years. When he was old enough to refuse conversion to the official Christian religion however, they found themselves pushed even further along the Mediterranean and eventually into the Western Roman Empire just as it was falling.

The area of Northern Italy in which they hoped to finally settle fell under the control of bandits before the self appointed first king of Italy, Flavius Odacar brought some order back. But that was almost a year after the child emperor, Romulus Augustus was deposed. The two lost both parents and an uncle to bandit tribes and he spent the last of their money paying a ransom for Tara's release.

Once targeted by these marauders however, it was only a matter of time before such a profitable kidnapping would be repeated, so they continued west and north through the Southern Alps and into Gaul. Once there, they were fortunate to join up with a stream of internally displaced refugees, including Yoan and his wife Zabrine. Whole villages were being displaced by Huns who'd taken advantage of Rome's collapse by crossing the Danube. Yoan took them under his wing as they moved ever further northwest and eventually found themselves in Armorica. Ignatius had never heard of Armorica but since no-one else was curious about it, he just listened.

Once there, they met up with Danel. His story didn't cover quite as many time zones but his journey was no less tragic. Apparently Gallaecia stretched along much of northern Iberia, though Satyan had also mentioned another Iberia on the Black Sea as the source of his barbarians. The fact that there were two of these entities was news to Ignatius but then, so was much of what he learned that night.

Danel claimed that he lived in a Christian community following the teachings of a bishop named Priscillian. Priscillian was from the same region but he lived almost a hundred years previously. The bishop was executed by order of the Pope of the time who declared him a heretic. Danel made the point that the pope together with a number of influential Italian bishops contrived a charge of sorcery, whereas their differences, according to him, were purely matters of religious interpretation. A Roman General named Maximus carried out the sentence and forcefully eradicated most of the original Priscillian community in southern Gallaecia.

What was left of what Ignatius would have called a sect, elected to live in quiet religious autonomy and severed all contacts with Rome and eventually reestablished the community into which Danel was born. However, it seemed that no part of the old world was immune to land grabs from beyond the borders of previous Empires. Visigoths were already established in the south of the country that would become Spain and they pushed north to take possession of most of it. It was inevitable that they would stumble into one of Danel's peaceful tribal communities.

The Priscillian Christians were no match for the battle hardened Visigoths and fled north to the sea. They skirted the Bay of Biscay coast into Gaul but because they were considered heretics, they found few friends there.

Where there was no fear of retribution from provincial rulers allied to the Roman Church, there was death at the hands of the Huns. In the lawless territories loyal to no-one or still being fought over, they had to improve their fighting skills and enlist mercenaries to protect the women and children from slavery and worse. They discovered that even the best mercenaries turn unreliable when money runs short.

As with Satyan before him, Danel named more names than Ignatius could hope to remember later. The upshot however, was that most of their community was lost or scattered between the Pyrenees and a place he called Soisson.

When they met up with Yoan and his wife, together with Satyan and his sister in Armorica, they were already preparing to leave the province. An influx of British Celts comprising Roman Christians and what he called ‘the old religions’ were feuding amongst themselves and the original settlers for jurisdiction over the area. Some of those northern refugees were reputedly running from the forces of Auxerre, acting on instructions from Rome, as well as from bands of Saxons. The Saxons and their allies were moving gradually westwards across ancient Britain from their original landfalls in the east.

Coincidentally, all six found themselves retracing the journey that Priscillian the heretic bishop had himself taken, before he was captured and executed almost a hundred years before. They landed in the Scilly Isles, which was a busy staging post for Britons on route to Armorica, and Ignatius made the connection between Armorica and its later name of Brittany.

The Scilly Isles also marked the western boundary of the Cornish Kingdom and piracy was a way of life for many, even back then. There was no shortage of dishonest business opportunities amongst the desperate and disorganised flows of humanity. Danel and his group managed to hire a boat to take them on to Munster and they thought they'd finally arrived when they literally bumped into the Scelec in a fog that lasted two full days and a night.

The telling of his story was like reliving it for Danel and once done, he sat with his head lowered and shoulders shuddering, sobbing for the loss of so many. Suivne and himself seemed to have grown quite close and the monk was doing his best to console him. Regaining some composure, he told them that his daughter Oinah, who was apparently the young girl Ignatius had seen helping Tara and Zabrine, was the sole survivor of their community. That was, he explained, because he'd died countless times before reaching Scelec.

It was not lost on Ignatius that these six refugees from the far corners of the old world represented the tip of an iceberg of countless others lost to the turbulence of the age. Most significant to the priest however, was the common enemy exacerbating the attrition suffered from savage invasions. It was the Church to which he'd dedicated his previous life.

"You are testing me, Ignatius." For the third time in a day he'd brought a scowl to the king's face.

"I do apologise, King Dooah. I haven't heard so much tragedy in my life and I can only imagine the suffering of our friends here who came through it." He was lost for words but Dooah was impatient for his story.

"We are all waiting to see how your travels compare to theirs." He insisted.

Dooah's impatience caused him to rush unprepared into an incomplete story. "I thought my tragedy began after I was ordained a priest and my mother asked me to say Mass in our family home. That's because my brother died during the offering."

"Offering? Mass? Died from what?" Dooah cutting him short so soon showed that despite the late hour, storytelling was not simply a passing of time. It was a formal ceremony in which some details were of far more importance than others. It came to him then that he hadn't moved and was still physically in Ireland, but was so far from attuned its civilisation. Here, it was he who was savage.

Realising his mistake, Ignatius explained. "It's a Christian ceremony that recalls the sacrifice of Jesus." He offered.

"Jesus is Yeshua, your god?" Asked Dooah, leaning forward.

"Yes." He said, seeing no reason to complicate the issue.

“And yours?” The king pointed at Suivne, who nodded, and then to Danel, who also nodded. “- and you, Satyan?”

“I can’t say for sure Sir, but that could be.” Said the younger man.

Dooah seemed far more puzzled than he should have been and Ignatius waited for approval to proceed with his story, but it didn’t come.

“It’s part of my vocation as a god anointed King to make enemies of no god and to learn all ceremonies of civilised appeasement to them. So I already know something about Yeshua, just as I do about the other gods and not just those of these islands, but this is the first time I have heard of Mass. Do you light a bonfire and make a feast?” He asked earnestly.

“No, Sir. Remembering Jesus, or Yeshua at Mass can be done any day and even every day. It is a fundamental duty for every Christian to take part in Mass at least once every seven days.”

The King looked at Suivne who shrugged at first, but then seemed to find his voice. “At the last supper, before he was crucified, Yeshua told his followers to eat bread and drink wine in his memory.” Said the monk. His voice rising like a proposal awaiting acceptance.

“Is that Mass?” Asked Dooah.

“Yes Sir.” Said Ignatius with a broad smile, which Dooah returned with interest.

“I always keep some good wine at Ventry and I will have some delivered tomorrow, so we can have a Mass here after the fasting.” He knew that he would need all the help he could get to win a war with Cashel. Being in a position to placate three gods in the same number of days was an opportunity not be wasted.

“But Sir, I can’t say Mass. Firstly, we don’t have a consecrated stone to use as an altar and secondly, my Bishop has revoked my authority to say Mass until I’ve accepted god back into my life. Lastly, the Mass is only for Christians. Your reverence for Dagda and Lugh is no secret and in this room there are people who profess to be Christians but who don’t seem to behave accordingly.” Once freed, words are not redeemable and his hung in the silence for an inordinately long time before being muted and then chilled by stone.

It was bewildering to see Dooah’s face cycle from outrage to the kind of look a father might show an errant child. “And have you accepted your god back into your life, Ignatius?”

“Yes, Sir, I have.” He realised his mistake too late and Dooah took only a moment to reflect on it.

“Scelec Tearmann has been consecrated ground from the day it first broke the surface of the endless sea to bridge the vastness between this mortal world and the next. Any god who would refuse prayers from a place as pure as this is not a god worth kneeling to."

The sputtering light of the single animal fat candle was bright enough to show Dooah's face redden, but it continued to darken further.

"Did it somehow escape you that I, Dooah Dairinne, am King in Munster?" It was shot at the priest as accusation and insult combined.

"This is not Rome, which means there will never be a bishop here with more authority than his king. Since you are now reconciled with your god, I authorise you to perform a mass right here." Tara caught the king's eye with a small hand gesture.

He acknowledged the dark girl's subtle moderation and took a few moments to gather his thoughts. The priest had told them he was a well travelled teacher and as such, he probably presumed to know more than some minor king at the edge of the world. He took a deep breath and proceeded in more measured tones.

"I regard Suivne as a good Christian because he lives according to the words of his 'Vetus Latina' and not those of some pompous pope or his bishops. He also reads it to me so that I too, can learn something of the 'Messiah' they call Yeshua. I have read not once but many times that the purpose of Yeshua was to offer himself as a perfect sacrifice that would bring the gods closer to everyone everywhere. In a way, his offering was like Tearmann, in that it would bridge the vastness between gods and men by removing the 'so called' holy of holies that separates them. Yeshua's sacrifice destroyed the impenetrable curtain that divides men from their gods. Am I right, so far?"

The tone suggested a loaded question, but despite the plurality of his gods, it was also pretty much the simple truth. Suivne was just as keen to see him nod and he looked towards the monk.

"Suivne's interpretation of the book compares well to my own beliefs, Sir." He was tempted to reduce the quantity of Dooah's gods to one, but then anticipated problems selling the concept of the Christian Trinity.

Something stopped him from feeling too smug about this opportunity to follow his vocation by spreading his 'Good News', and Ignatius was gobsmacked. Fortunately for him, Dooah didn't follow up with the logical conclusion, which spoke volumes about his character. But Danel harboured no such finesse and stood up.

"It follows then that if someone can't commune with his god without a priest and if a priest needs the authority of a bishop and a bishop the anointing of a pope, who can make no mistake when he claims to represent god directly, then Yeshua wasted more than just his life."

Ignatius was horrified to find that he had no answer for that, but Danel wasn't quite finished. "So, either the greatest sacrifice ever made was pointless, or Rome's corrupt clerics replaced the curtain that Yeshua shredded with countless others of their own making." He paused for only a second. "That makes you, Ignatius, the only true heretic here."

Ignatius was stunned but only Dooah seemed aware of the conflict breaking into spontaneous combustion inside him. He only vaguely heard the king speak.

"You may sit down Danel and you, Ignatius, may examine your conscience later. However, you can console yourself with the thought that you are not the only heretic cleric here. Tearmann seems to collect them lately." He chuckled at that, even with all of the assembled heretics so obviously unimpressed.

"Right now," he went on, "- the hour is late and my bed calls, but I will hear you finish your story."

Dooah was probably the most unlikely of discerning people he'd come across. This least regal of kings had plunged his so recently reordered world back into chaos by dissecting one word, Mass. It exposed the fallacy of dedicating his pointless life to anything. Ignatius knew that anything he chose to say was sure to be another mistake, but neither silence nor lies were options. A primitive, oversized ragamuffin that he'd taken for a giant grunt was indeed a king and he could see right through him.

The priest struggled to find a word worthy of a new beginning for his story. That search was hampered by a highly trained, finely tuned and supposedly pious character who also struggled with an accusation of heresy, levelled by an acknowledged heretic. Deception was simply beyond his multi-tasking capabilities, though he would have to omit some awkward details.

So, he told them about his father's death coming so soon after his brother's heart attack and then about his mother and finally, his stricken sister. Then he told them something about his recovery in the care of a foreign born Brother, Chaz.

"Like Suivne?" Dooah enquired. He was interested enough in people to want more than just a name.

"Yes, Sir but he's built more like you and with skin the colour of midnight." That brought the king's smile back. He liked Chaz already but then, he'd be in the very good company of many. He came quickly to the section of road with the missing wall, where he'd fallen off Skellig Michael and took an age to hit cold water.

"When?" No-one could say that Dooah didn't have a knack of getting to the crux of a matter.

"I believe it was this same day. The day between the two fasts. Where I come from, it would be called Thursday."

"Suivne told me as much about the day Ignatius, but when was that day?" He was like a terrier with a bone and wasn't about to let it go.

“I don’t know for sure, Sir, but it seems that I didn’t just fall down … I also fell backwards in time.” The weight lifting from his shoulders left him slightly giddy, but relief was brief when he remembered the impact at the end of that plunge followed by another near death experience in the cold embrace of the sea. Men like Dooah didn’t suffer fools lightly and a single word could see it reenacted, from higher.

Tara wasn’t oblivious to his dilemma. “Tell the king when that fall will happen.” The way she reworded the king’s question made the fact of his dilemma somewhat insignificant. The critical point was her acceptance that someone could just materialise from the future and all she wanted to know was the date of his fall.

“I can only guess the year because the same calendar is not used here, but I believe a good estimate would make it a millennium and a half from now.”

While Tara and Dooah exchanged knowing glances Ignatius waited to be led out of the little stone hut and unceremoniously hurled into the darkness around Skellig, possibly with his throat slit so as not to disturb the storyteller’s telling of ‘The Tain’.

“Then it didn’t all finish like the mad Bishop Patricius says it will.” Suivne muttered it like he’d heard nothing more unusual than rain was in the forecast.

“What’s not finished?” Asked the priest, relieved to be still breathing but amazed at how readily such an incredible story could be accepted by such superstitious people.

“It means that the end times of ‘Revelations’ won’t arrive, despite our belief that we are now living through them.” Said Satyan and Yoan added what had to be an obscenity, though in a language he couldn’t understand.

“QUIET!” Commanded Dooah and he waited until all eyes were on him.

“Magus Tara told me that Ignatius was not from this time, which means he came through a ‘Thin Place’ or he was sent here by magic. Our lore contains many stories of people and things that come and go from this world without being nursed into it or leaving it on a funeral pyre, but how did you know, Tara?” He looked to his left.

“Did you need your magic to see where, or when he came from?” Asked the king.

“I needed only my eyes.” Her latin was easily as rudimentary as her brother’s, but she was more in tune with the subject and not overly concerned with her grammar. It was like pigin-latin, but she knew their latin was such that she could be understood. “No-one can stitch the bottom of a shoe to the top with the same stitch size every single time.” She said quietly.

“What?” Ignatius heard his own voice hit a pitch that he’d never heard himself reach before.

Satyan spoke up to help them understand his sister. “What Tara is saying is a machine with,” he struggled for the right word, "-calibration is needed, and we have only begun to make use of such tools in Persia, mainly for farming and irrigation.”

“Yes.” Said Tara. “But a world more than a millennium from now is too far away for me to imagine.” She followed with. “Tell us something of our world to be.” Then she looked squarely at Ignatius.

“NO!” Dooah was emphatic.

“I forbid questions about the future because knowing such things will change what we do today and tomorrow. The gods are sure to be angered if they discover that we know their intentions. People will stop praying and maybe even prevent destiny if they think they know what the future holds. And if people stop praying to them, we can only guess what the gods might do to us in return.”

He pointed accusingly at Ignatius. “You have arrived amongst us with very dangerous information. Your life is all the evidence we need that the end times don’t arrive and that means that equilibrium must still be possible but only if you don’t speak of it.”

Then with quiet authority. “Do you all understand what I’ve just said?”

“But surely he can answer one question, please Dooah, - just one.” It was Suivne.

“We need to know what will happen to our Persia.” Demanded Satyan.

“Will Gallaecia survive the Visigoths?” Danel shouted.

“NO!” Insisted Dooah. When their debate broke down into a shouting match, the king spread his hands and silently demanded order.

It arrived in stages but he was patient and when he spoke he was quietly collected. “If we allow the first question, it will be followed by the second and then a third. We are all from different parts of this world, which will mean more questions and an even greater chance of change to what all of us plan to do tomorrow. I tell you now that if we don’t agree on this matter, you will leave me no option but to kill Ignatius.”

A disconnected laugh followed by a child’s cry and small applause filtered in to fill the stunned silence of a room that looked more like a cave. The priest however, was horrified by how glibly his death was thrown into a simple proposal.

When the noisy debate found new wind to resurrect itself, Dooah knew they weren't convinced that he wouldn't flinch from what he considered his duty.

"You know very well Suivne, that not every monk in Munster is Christian." And Suivne nodded slowly in agreement.

"Part of the king's function is ensuring harmony between men and their gods and if only a human sacrifice will do that, then so be it, and I will see it done."

For a Christian monk, Suivne then showed an immoral disregard for the priest's life by further pursuing the matter. "No-one can debate the wisdom of those words, King Dooah. We certainly don't want any of the gods to be so displeased with us, that they punish us like some who've been washed up on this shore. However, there is an opportunity here for knowledge that could be useful against our common enemy."

"What do you mean?" Asked Dooah dourly.

"As you said, Scelec Tearmann is not a strategic place. People have fought on this rock as recently as this morning, but we were not fighting for possession of it. It's not something that's fought over. Your people, the Tuatha Dairinne have from time before time, used Tearmann as an altar, simply because it's so much closer to the gods.

"I am tired Suivne, please make your point."

"Of course Dooah, of course." Suivne continued briskly.

"Everyone has seen that the Roman Church considers it a sacred duty to desecrate all other altars by either destroying them, or by decorating them with their own idols and images. So, if they ever get control of Munster, then it stands to reason that they would build another sacrilegious altar here. If we can just ask Ignatius that one and only question, then his answer will tell most of us all we need to know about our respective futures, - and especially yours, Sir."

The wizened old man sitting next to him tugged the king's arm and they had a short whispered conversation that ended with Dooah jolted upright.

"Rudgael tells me that he doesn't want to know when or how he will die. He says it is everyone's duty to fight for their last breath or for survival, and I agree. If a king accepts death believing it destiny, then he risks failing far more than just himself."

It was clear however that he was tempted by Suivne's suggestion, because a long silence endured until Dooah decided to stifle it once and for all.

"Scelec Tearmann has always been a special place for all people and for all their gods, even those who've not yet revealed themselves to us. That's why Dairinne Kings have placed such importance on its protection and I take that sacred duty very seriously. However, people who pray must have protection before the altars they pray from. If I am to be the last Dairinne King then let that be also, but I must fight to the end for what I believe."

He raised his cup and took a slow draught. "I don't believe in hearsay, and it is because I have felt an awesome presence all around this place that I know a supreme god protects Tearmann with me. I believe this god will continue to keep it pure if ever or whenever the last king dies. So, I don't need to know if the mad bishop, Patricius, will build one of his altars here or not. I know that if he does then a greater power will take it down to keep Tearmann pure for all the gods."

He looked at both Ignatius and Suivne in turn and the priest's stomach lurched when the monk pointed accusingly at him. "But this priest is not your people Dooah, nor is he our people. However, if he is telling the truth about his fall from the future, then he has information that could save the lives of many of us." He wasn't finished gambling with a life that wasn't his own.

"No-one will leave Tearmann until this issue is resolved and believe me, it will be, but only after I have prayed aloft and completed tomorrow's fast. Meanwhile, Ignatius may not speak to anyone about anything. If his next words are not to me tomorrow, they will be his last."

Without another word, Dooah dismissed the small gathering by ushering everyone outside. As they left, a bulky man who'd apparently been loitering discreetly outside, took his cue to enter. With the last of them outside, they saw him struggle through the narrow entrance with a number of thick furs slung over both shoulders and another rolled under his arm. He then started laying them on the slab behind Dooah. It was only when he'd finished making up Dooah's bed that he could be seen for the whippet-like teenager he really was.

"We should meet again tomorrow when we can talk freely and while Dooah is not here with us." Said Suivne, showing them his extremely stubborn agenda.

Ignatius couldn't help but wonder just how serious Dooah was in summarily silencing him. He was about to ask the monk who, as his adopted son, knew the king better than anyone else. However, Tara touched him lightly on the shoulder as she passed. She smiled serenely but placed a cool finger on his lips and kept it there until he nodded.

"We are all free to meet and talk as we wish Suivne, but Ignatius has decided to take Dooah's advice and will also pray and fast." Then she turned with a rustle of her long robe and with her brother in tow.

12 - URNEE (Prayer)

Despite the late hour, his hyperactive mind had no intention of releasing him. The bonfire was reduced to a source of barely visible heat, a wide pile of dark red ash that glowed momentarily when the breeze remembered to visit. Brightness then became relative as he watched with his back against the perimeter wall, until only an occasional spark showed where the bonfire once was. Those fortunate enough to have designated sleeping areas, weather protected or not, found their way to them. That left him with the problem of not stepping on sleeping bodies whenever he decided to make his way to his own.

As an educated foreigner and therefore a VIP, Ignatius could enjoy his strip of sleeping space at the back of the men's beehive hut, next to the one designated as a make-shift hospital ward. However, that would oblige him to speak to others. Tara had surprised him with her wordless warning to stay silent, but there was someone he could always talk to.

He needed to pray but mainly because it was a pre-conditioned prelude to any Examen. Praying was what Jesuits did to get into the spiritual 'zone', but he was no longer sure that Jesus would still hear him. He climbed over the wall to face a smear of light seeping in from the East and once again leaned against the wall to think.

He recalled his introduction to 'Higher Level' Catechism classes when he was just twelve years old. His teacher told him to consider it a promotion from childhood into the ranks of soldiers for god and that idea stuck, but then what kid didn't fancy himself as a soldier at some stage? He could still see Father Anthony's sad saggy eyes well-up as he imparted the words of the Saints, Paul to Augustine, to a class that secularism would reduce year on year, until only two students remained. "Bis orat qui bene cantat", whoever sings well prays twice.

Those religious doctrine classes started as a punishment for doing absolutely nothing wrong and he had to confess to taking them quite badly at first. Especially when the other boys got to play games and then boast of their freedom to do so. The thing was, his mother took more pleasure in his religion classes than he could, so like a good Mama's boy, he persevered to keep her happy.

His Mama ruled their humble home and had somehow clung to the archaic notion that a Catholic Mother's duty was to produce a priest, a teacher, a soldier or a policeman and a banker. The fact that such naivety had survived the millennium was nothing short of mind blowing. Nevertheless, his sister was a primary school teacher before she fell ill, though his older brother had apparently failed his mother. So eventually, prayer for Ignatius became the curiosity of a Zen-like duty, not dissimilar to chants from saffron-robed monks who didn't have a real god to believe in.

He soon learned that Buddhism was more of a philosophy than a genuine religion and dismissed it as such. There was however, something really special about Gregorian Chanting, and especially when it was live and inside a great cathedral. That was an experience that few people outside of the clergy could share. Plebs would have to satisfy themselves with digital recordings or maybe a reasonable Gospel Choir. At the bottom of the scale, there would always be the periodic treat of sacramental incense and a good instrumental on a church organ, though these were getting cheaper by the day. On his studious travels, he found that he was particularly susceptible to the aphrodisiacal opiate of a real pipe organ in the hands of a maestro.

He shivered at the thought of that incredible New Year's Eve recital and even the memory could still reduce him to tears. He was on his knees looking east, like a Muslim facing Mecca and after considerable thought, dismissed it as an unsuitable direction for his prayers. Islam's Quran boldly states that if the seas were ink, there would still be insufficient to write down all the names of god, yet arcane words directed at Mecca get precedence. With no music, no song or singing, he was himself reduced to using the words of ready made mantras for the masses. They held little in the way of spiritual exhilaration, but they were specifically designed to appease the one true god … of Rome.

The Roman Church he was sworn to serve, for life and for his dead mother's delight, had through the infallible dogma of Edicts and Encyclicals, Diets, Synods and Conventions, exiled god for everyone except those already perfect. Penances, indulgences and sacraments just added to countless distortions of the Word, so he looked up.

Pinpoints of starlight, some travelling from the birth of the universe, bounced back into space from his black irises to begin the long journey back. Some planets still shone, but galaxies of stars would soon be banished by imminent dawn.

"But they will still shine behind the blue light of day because it will be a long time before night falls for everyone, everywhere." He mused, only slightly surprised by the minor revelation that when all light eventually disappears from the universe, life must surely follow.

"Yes," He agreed. "- in maybe another whatever trillion years." He couldn't remember the precise figure and dismissed it, like Buddhism and Islam, wondering what had provoked such a strange train of thoughts.

"Strange?" If they were spoken words, they would have been whispered but even a whisper was talking. He took a quick look around and then wondered why he'd bothered to do such a stupid thing.

"If you find such thoughts strange then shouldn't you consider that maybe I'm not you after all?"

"Of course you're me. You're my alter ego, my higher mind and I'm just afraid of being overheard, that's all."

"And there was me thinking you were mine. Anyway, how do you propose we file away the little secret of your fall from grace?"

"I dismissed that earlier, when I learned there was no grace to fall from." After considerable thought, he'd decided to make sense of that long fall into more primitive times by seeing it as his own fall from grace, like another angel falling from paradise for sins of disobedience.

He followed up with. "It's all bullshit now isn't it?" He really didn't want to talk about it now.

"Well, that depends on you."

"How?" This was getting a bit crazy. He laughed … out loud, or so he thought and then had to take another nervous look around.

"It's OK Ignatius. I won't tell Dooah when he comes calling later today that you spoke out of turn." Now that was funny.

Time is not constant. It goes faster the closer you get to a gravitational mass. But it can also go faster when you simply lose track of it. Bands of high cirrus cloud glowed grey at first and then deep red like the dying fire but in reverse. They glowed steadily brighter, and then brighter still until his squinting eyes hurt.

"If that pale blue sky between the clouds was a distant calm sea, there would be one sea facing up and another facing down. And if those clouds were islands at sunset, or sunrise, then one of them could be Skellig facing down while your Skellig faces up. Two realities facing off against each other for the right to be real." Suggested the voice adding. "But which one?"

Ignatius had done this before, though many years ago when there seemed to be plenty of time to soak up those halcyon summer sunsets on fire as he lay on the beach or the grass. He could see the same effect above.

"Yes." He said. "I remember looking up at those islands like I was flying over them, but really high, maybe even from orbit. He could see that some of the clouds even had inlets, like small sheltered bays in paradise isles."

He remembered one time in particular when the illusion was made complete with the thin taper of a jet trail close to the horizon and between a number of 'golden islands'. He saw it as a wake left in the pale blue ocean by a resident or a visitor to that otherworldly paradise who seemed to have it all to himself, and he wanted to be the lucky one.

"Don't you think it strange that even back then, you never considered falling down from up there, especially since your much vaulted fall from grace was actually quite puny by comparison.” It was said with more than a touch of suggestion.

The voice in his head went on. “Then again, you’d probably have to be up there to consider falling down here and if you were, then surely the reverse of a fall is ascent.”

Ignatius couldn’t be sure when it began because it was almost imperceptible until he felt lightheaded and then his stomach fluttered slightly. He looked down to eliminate the unthinkable but his feet were already above the grass. He could no longer stay silent but his cry came out like the screech of a gull.

13 - RITES

They stood side by side on the precipice, just a handful of steps behind the stone beehive huts. To his left was the near vertical drop from the higher southern peak into a sea speckled with roving white dots that were gannets, kittiwakes and puffins far below. Dooah had just returned from spending the day alone and at the top of that natural and yet unnatural spire. Pristine splendour from horizon to horizon would have humbled the much lesser mortal that Ignatius was, before the out of body experience of his perfect prayer. Just then however, he was a part of it and just soaked the rest of it in. He still had some way to go in coming down from the high of that most powerful of narcotics.

Skellig was still draped in shades of sunrise gold but after the longest night, came the shortest and practically timeless day, and they were facing west towards sunset. Long sword held horizontal as an offering, Dooah's right thumb caressed the bronze hilt guard while the thumb of his left brushed across the blade from one side to the other.

"For you great Dagda." Said the king loudly and he hefted the sword over his head. He then created an arc with the tip until it was slicing the air with a whistle. With practised precision, it was released at the optimum point of the throw and a satisfied grunt followed it. From such a great height, the sword seemed to somersault away and then down in slow motion. That gave them longer to count the flashes of reflected sunset it threw back up at them as it went.

"For you, Lord." The little crucifix had neither the mass nor inertia to parallel the sword's trajectory through the golden sky, so it disappeared rather disappointingly into a background of sea, heather and then white guano-caked outcrops. However, a coin is a poor man's fortune and an offering is an offering, so they both watched until they were sure it was gone, or rather accepted, somewhere between sky and sea.

Touch down was as gentle as take-off, but falling to earth at any speed was enough to jolt him awake at the same spot he'd apparently fallen asleep. He lay exactly where he'd planned to welcome the dawn, but the sun had already passed over the wall behind him and so he lay in its shadow. The only evidence of his astral travels were the trembles still radiating out from his core, and they rendered him speechless for a time. When they eventually dissipated, he was grossly disappointed to re-discover he was merely mortal once again.

Timing is everything and the king chose pretty much the moment of his recovery to send a runner out to find him. He was quite simply invited to face the sunset and the future together. When Ignatius proposed his solution, the king didn't need to summon witnesses to a cleric's submission or to his own superior status in accepting it. With a minimum of ceremony, he bent his knee to the King of Munster and undertook to obey any and all of his just commands before all others, regardless of where they might come from.

“I do.” He said simply, when asked.

“And in return, I will serve you and your interests to the best of my ability.” Said Dooah and that was that.

Business concluded, he proceeded with his sword offering. When it was done, Ignatius was tempted to put Dooah at ease and tell him that he was right. Skellig would only suffer Rome’s mandatory altars temporarily. A complete monastery would be built, but then be subjected to Viking raids and abductions and eventually, after an unusually prolonged spell of inclement weather, the bishop of the time would be obliged to permanently relocate his monks to the mainland. However, the king was still somebody and he’d undertaken not to speak to anyone about the future, so he held his tongue.

That was probably just as well, because he would reflect on that particular milestone in his life some days later. He would wonder what it would have taken for Dooah to make a very different sacrifice that evening.

Just then however, his mind was only barely back in the real world but even so, he’d anticipated what would happen next.

"They've brought us some wine and that bread is still hot from the oven. Since we've both fasted and prayed, you can now say Mass before we eat." With two gods happy and soon to be joined by a third, and with the status quo restored, he was content to release the words in the form of a request.

The sky was already a bright shade of violet when they joined the small congregation of royalty, heretics, pagans and representatives of the miscellaneous masses assembled not far below it.

"For you … Brother." Suivne handed him a quickly crafted cross of half burned wood salvaged from the edge of the fire, then filed and smoothed into shape.

"Scorched hardwood is fully seasoned and it will last much longer." He added, when Ignatius raised it to his lips and then hesitated when his nose registered delicate hints of wood-smoke. There was no image mounted on it and it wasn't worthy of any self respecting carpenter anywhere, but Ignatius was elated to have it and he received it graciously.

"I'll never be separated from it … Brother."

There were still too many people to fit into the biggest Beehive, which was in any case reserved for Dooah while he was there. His Majesty had already taken the liberty of appointing his grandson altar boy. Dallan was delighted with the honour and wiped the cleanest wooden cup with a dirty looking rag before placing it on an altar that was as uneven as a miniature Dolmen.

The Council of Trent would formally establish the format for mass to ensure that it wasn't personalised or revised by overly zealous, if well meaning clerics. But by the time Ignatius was ordained priest, the detail and dogma applied to its recital alone, would require an allocation of study time and effort similar to that of an entire thesis. With his torn shirt and a fox-fur thrown over his shoulders and with no vestments or girdle, he could expect nothing less than excommunication for his imminent blasphemy.

Disregarding countless right foot, left foot, right hand and left hand with turn right turn left protocols, he approached the unconsecrated altar only too well aware that he also had no upper vestments, no chasuble, stole nor maniple. Those would be colour coded for use at specific mass rites, such as marriages and funerals. They also identified different times and events of the liturgical year.

The dynamics of day being quickly overtaken by night deepened the sky to a darker shade of violet that matched the official colour of humility. Ignatius thought that was particularly apt and prepared to continue in latin. This was a language that was at different religious times banned, then mandatory, then subject to restrictions until it was tolerated for mass once more, though a number of provisos applied.

His version of mass veered away from the established tradition after just two words, "In Nomine…", after which he replaced the Trinity of Father, Son and Holy Spirit, with "Yeshua."

Then he switched back to the official text. "Judica me, Deus etc, (Judge me God and distinguish my cause from those of an ungodly nation: Deliver me from an unjust and deceitful enemy.)" That done, he abandoned the mandatory texts and ad-libbed his way through what he thought might be a reasonable reenactment of the last supper of Jesus.

When he came to his final 'Amen', he suffered another involuntary tremble but it was one of exhilaration and elation when a great weight was cast off like a demon, and his soul threatened to soar once more.

"It can't be a sin anyway." He said casually to himself after saying Skellig's first ever Mass.

"True." He had to agree because they both knew that the Council of Trent that would define the dogmatic aspects of 'Mass', was still more than a millennium away.

14 - SCHEMES

She was crying when she came out, even though she carried a very elaborate brooch that was more of a status symbol than something practical to fasten her Sunday-Best cloak. Her attempted smile was too brief and when she came up to him she turned her face down feigning closer scrutiny of her prize.

She held it long enough for him to see it was made of bronze and it easily filled the palm of her open hand. Two birds were mounted on it and they were clearly made of mounted gold. Their wings and the delicate swirls from the wingtips that then entwined them were silver in contrast. Beak to beak, two intensely blue eyes that could have been sapphires were raised high enough to look out and also into each other. She had a curious way of flipping it over, but she didn't wait long enough for him to see the reverse because she just ran off. He'd have to talk to her later.

Just then, a thick overcast began spitting heavier rain from the drizzle that began before dawn. Aside from a heavily armed attendant cum bodyguard and his two grandsons, Suivne, Tara, Danel and Ignatius were the only people left in the high compound on Skellig. The monk had his audience first and was followed by the Magus, as he called her. Now it was his turn. Dooah sat alone in the centre of the same stone slab that he'd used during the story telling on Lughnasa.

“There is a change of weather on the wind and my boat lies off Tearmann’s Northside. They say if I don’t get down there soon, the crew will have no choice but to leave me behind.” He laughed at his own joke, which also meant that he’d also enjoyed his breakfast.

“So, I’ll be very brief, Ignatius.”

“Yes Sir.” He said formally.

“I will need you to follow me to Munster and then travel north to counter the …” he struggled to find the right word, “- propaganda of the mad Bishop, Patricius. He uses two weapons to convert the ignorant and superstitious to the Roman Church. They are the threat of his Armageddon Revelations and if that doesn’t work, he then threatens them with Armageddon from an army from Rome, which he claims is only a few days away. Because we are by nature a simple and fearful people, his tactics work only too well.”

“As you wish, Sir.” Because he was capable of death by drowning and also by sword having also experienced hunger, thirst and fear, he had to accept that he was where he obviously was. However, the thought of confronting Saint Patrick on scriptural interpretation, took some moments to digest.

“Have you some difficulty with that, Ignatius? It seems you have little to say to me now, yet most times you can’t seem to keep your mouth shut.”

“No Sir. Suivne and I are in full agreement that Jesus, or rather Yeshua clearly states that his ‘Revelations’ were details of changes that would take place shortly after his death. Yoan, Danel, Tara and the others survived those changes but countless others did not. The fall of Rome and invasions from all fronts into old empires are simply ‘Revelations’ coming to pass. The promised new age can only come when this one is fully closed and the reason I have little to say, is because I know something about the Bishop that could make my job difficult. Though that won’t stop me from doing my utmost.”

He waited for a moment before adding. “I don’t have possessions, so I’m ready to leave now if that’s what you have in mind.”

The thought of leaving Skellig on a mission that must ultimately fail didn’t fill him with joy. But it wasn’t like he had other things to do, like finding like minded souls to enlist in the cause. He could only look forward to the limited personal satisfaction of putting a couple of things right, even though the overall outcome was historically assured. His mischievous mind was busy creating an image of St. Patrick in impossibly expensive emerald and gold robes. He was cursing in Gaelic while wielding a hooked shillelagh to drive out snakes and heretic Jesuits. All totally inappropriate but difficult to dispel.

"There is a time for everything," he said smiling, "- and first I will send you some inks and vellum so you can fully prepare your testaments. Personally, I can't understand the Christian compulsion to battle letters with more letters. Even my adopted son Suivne is intent on writing his …" again he dug deep to find the appropriate word, "- memoirs. So, after some thought, I'm leaving you here for a time so you can help him. He envies your latin, you see."

"That will be my pleasure." He said, but his comment didn't appear to please his king.

"I'm sure it will." Said Dooah thoughtfully, adding. "It wasn't an easy decision to make. I had planned to take you with me, but there are some intricate details that need my attention first. I will send for you in due course and when I do, you will probably find that Magus Tara will want to accompany you and she is always free to do as she wishes. In the meantime, I have no option but to leave her here under your protection." He stood up and Ignatius found himself dismissed rather prematurely.

"She seemed quite upset as she was leaving. Is there something the rest of us should know … Sir?"

Dooah regarded him steadily for a few moments, perhaps weighing his loyalty, or his trustworthiness with state secrets.

"You will not speak of this to anyone but Tara has received a proposition and a gift from my son, Crochur. If anything happens to me, he will give our kingdom continuity but he is not quite his father. He will need a strong educated wife who knows something of the world outside to set him above other contenders. So I've instructed her to marry him and it seems she needs some time to get accustomed to the idea, that's all." He strapped his scabbard to a thick leather belt and then felt the weight of his new sword before sliding it inside, where it didn't quite go all the way in.

"We must all get accustomed to new situations as they arise, Ignatius. You will find that life can be as difficult as it is precarious out here when the weather closes. So, Danel has asked me to take his young daughter with me as my ward. Yoan and his wife have already left, which means that Tara is now the only woman on Scelec Tearmann and for some reason that I can't yet fathom, she seems quite fond of you. So in return for keeping his daughter safe, Danel will help you to watch over our future queen. You do know what I mean?"

It took him a few seconds to appreciate the implication, which also brought him some unexpected guilt. "So why don't you just take her with you?" He said, more as a reaction than a rational suggestion.

"You really don't know much about women do you, priest? If I just wanted her to warm someone's bed then that's exactly what I'd do and that's probably what she'd expect, but I believe I might get something more important from her by indulging her whims for a while."

Despite himself, his twinge of guilt turned to anger or maybe something closer to jealousy that she could just be married off to someone she obviously didn't like. However, there was nothing for her on Skellig and there was no denying that she belonged in a royal household, so he nodded his agreement.

"She's certainly seen the world beyond Munster and I'm sure she's no stranger to the custom of arranged marriages, but maybe it would be wise to let her meet your son first, so she can get to know him better." He suggested.

"She has seen much more than her brother says she has, and I haven't yet disposed of Rudgael as my advisor. So for now, you just do as I tell you." And with that, Dooah blustered through the empty doorway shouting to someone who might have been waiting outside and was gone.

He found Tara in the beehive next to the smallest one at the end. The two young boys had already commandeered that cell, claiming they could see more of the straits from inside it. He found that she'd recovered remarkably well and the only sign that she wasn't quite herself was her reluctance to meet his eyes.

"Does Satyan know?" Seemed to be a logical place to start.

She was quiet for a while. “His Majesty left that small task to me, otherwise there would have been big trouble, believe me. The problem is, if it came to blows my brother is no match for Dooah so there really was no choice …”

He had to admit that Dooah seemed to have thought the matter through quite thoroughly. “I tried to suggest that he let you meet the boy, sorry … Crochur first, but he didn’t take that very well.” He felt awkward talking about her impending marriage but also disappointed that the duty of consoling her had fallen to him. It was all very inappropriate despite the fact that the Jesuits had trained him to counsel.

“We were very lucky to get to Tearmann with our lives. We’ve both seen enough of the old world to turn our backs to it for good.” Her latin was basic and she didn’t differentiate between masculine and feminine nouns, but he didn’t care. She had eyes that were tantalisingly dangerous to hold for too long, though they easily held his.

“What do you mean?” He forced himself to ‘casually’ look away.

She sighed in resignation and then took a long deep breath and told him with a hand gesture to sit. “I do agree with Dooah that Scelec Tearmann is more than just beautiful but it's no place to settle.” She began.

“We’ve been here for some months now, but we’ve already seen how quickly things can change, even in summer. It will take something very special to survive a winter out here, which is why I knelt before him."

An involuntary "Aaahh" escaped him. It seemed that Dooah was not the only schemer in Munster.

She wasn't distracted. "My brother couldn't pledge his allegiance because the king is too obvious and makes no secret of his need to build an army. Satyan can handle a sword and is the equal of anyone his own size, but he wouldn't accept deployment that would take him away from me. He is protective, but I persuaded him to stay here while I scouted ahead onshore. I needed to see Munster in order to make our plans and move on, but this sea is endless and despite many rumours, there is no Atlantis to the West."

He was bound not to tell her that she was wrong about that, so he just waited for her to continue. "I've met a king and I've seen emperors and princes and neither Dooah nor his sons are anything like them and to be honest, Munster is a hovel compared to what we've seen, but the people welcome foreigners and it's also safer than anywhere we've been since Persia. There is also nowhere else to go."

Ignatius nodded in agreement. He knew that an Irish bronze-age provincial king would be nothing like King Arthur of the legends, and it followed that local princes were bound to have some rough edges. They also had few settlements which meant no castles, let alone palaces.

“From what I’ve seen, I know that this brooch represents a fortune in Munster, even though it comes from the hand of the father and not from his son. Also, life as a minor queen is probably the best I can achieve for both my brother and myself right now, but that doesn’t mean I have to be happy.” Her head dropped as she turned the brooch over from top to bottom rather than sideways.

After a while, he extended his hand and she passed the heavy ornament to him without a glance. The first thing that struck him about it was how warm she was.

“I asked him for time to think about it, but he knows we have nowhere else to go. He also knows better than anyone just how much time we have before we simply must leave this place.” She caught his eye and held it for two fleeting moments.

In the rain outside, someone was struggling with what sounded like pots and pans when a young mouth threw out a Gaelic obscenity. He’d picked up a few words here and there and was about to congratulate himself when he realised that most of what he’d learned were profanities. He needed to lift her spirits however, and was searching for a lighter subject when he remembered something else that Dooah had mentioned.

“The king suggested to me that you might have seen more than you were ready to admit to the rest of us.”

Her eyes swallowed him up again and the change of topic seemed to weigh heavily on her for a while, but he had nothing to do but wait. "You've seen the future Ignatius, and though you've promised not to speak of it, you spoke volumes to me while you were fighting your fevers." She smiled teasingly.

"But you can't speak that language. In fact, my mother tongue hasn't been spoken anywhere yet, so I'm very curious to know what you think you might have learned." He taunted her in return.

"I see things that most people can't and I'm also blessed with some very unusual gifts, Ignatius." She said it so softly that he had to lean nearer to hear. When he entered the perfumed bubble that followed her around, she dropped her voice even lower.

"When a feeling is expressed in any spoken word, patterns emerge over time and language was never a barrier to me reading minds and sometimes joining them. But my biggest gift or curse is seeing the past through lives already lived, through previous incarnations." His eyes popped open, but she didn't stay silent long enough for him to speak.

"I'm far from immortal but I am forever young, even though I've lived longer than anyone you've ever known. In those lives I've studied sciences like alchemy, though my greatest passion is healing. Knowledge accumulated over many short lifetimes is why Dooah calls me 'Magus' and why he wants me in Munster. I would have willingly accepted that strange destiny but lately, I've seen a problem in you." Her moist eyes sparkled with flashes of shadow and light from the doorway as people outside moved across it.

Tara was most definitely a very gifted healer but she was talking about immortality and even though he'd quite recently entertained similar notions about himself, he knew delusion when he saw it. So he made a subtle transition from patient and well-intended confidante to official counsellor.

"It seems you've learned far more about me than I know about myself. When I fell in here from the future, I couldn't possibly have imagined that you existed. So, I don't understand how I could suddenly present a problem." He was enjoying the impersonal and innocent diversion of the interaction, like patiently teasing secrets from a child who might not want to share them.

The novelty of such a simple game in times so turbulent should have appealed to her also, but reassembling intimate thoughts into unfamiliar words made it difficult for him to tell. When she arrived at what she wanted to say, the depth of her thinking surprised him.

"The strange thing about all those incarnations is the fact of so many lives cut short with no memories of a child in any of them. I am an oracle with empty pasts and then you fall into my world from a similarly childless future. The fact that lives end but that memories created in them live on regardless, has made me aware of other worlds that travel through time alongside ours or rather … mine. What that means is that I should know the difference between destiny and chance."

She paused before finishing. "And yet, we have both vowed allegiance to Munster."

He handed her brooch back while he tried to make sense of that riddle, convinced that her poor latin was complicating the discussion and so they sat silently out of the rain for some minutes. Ignatius thought he was beginning to understand when she simply resumed, like a bad internet connection that had been silently buffering in the background.

"If I could grant my own wish, I'd break this cycle of writing other people's destinies in place of achieving my own. If or when I revisit this life, there should be something worthwhile to review, like how I tried to reclaim my lost fortune and maybe some other things." She said at length, but like hearing a child ask for an impossible Christmas gift, he found no easy reply. He had to say something but he felt exposed and totally out of his depth.

"I know Munster must look primitive to you but these people are honest and sincere. I believe they will do anything to protect you long enough to raise a child." She looked like she wanted to smile but her head fell lower, covering what could be seen of her face with a sheen of black hair.

Ignatius dug deep for something to add. "Also, primitive doesn't mean that you won't have a warm bed and good food. You will still be a queen and that means servants. So why would you want to stay out here where it's not only dangerous but also extremely uncomfortable?"

When she swept her glossy mane back, her look was one of total exasperation.

"I'm beginning to believe that you were exorcised from the future because of your stupidity?"

It was only when she tried to laugh through her tears but failed miserably, that her full meaning hit home.

15 - HISPERICA FAMINA

Winter came hard, fast and far too early when they woke to horizontal hail in hurricane winds. By evening, it became a biblical deluge and the general weather pattern was set. This default was only occasionally interrupted with a day each of scudding skies, drizzle, rain, sleet and then a calm but frosty night or two.

Squeezed in between those nights, Skellig would be bathed in a lukewarm, light lemon sun for a few precious daylight hours during which a boat would magically arrive. Friendly faces would quickly deliver food, wood and also take requests for subsequent deliveries and yet, no summons came for Ignatius. Snatches of news were swapped before a hurried departure with whispered dispatches for Dooah from his grandsons.

The king had gone north to cement new alliances but every time the boys sighted a boat, Ignatius dreaded being called away from Skellig to join him. However, in three short months, even news of Dooah's diplomacy became stale like the bread, but Ignatius was obliged to remain on standby.

Danel wasted no time exercising his authority by dictating who slept where, with the exception of the two young boys, who outranked him from the smallest cell. He allocated the cell next to theirs to Tara and her brother with the third shared by the remaining men, Suivne, Ignatius and himself. Claiming that the sleeping area furthest from the door would offer more in the way of warmth while also discouraging draughts, he urged Ignatius to take it. Tara couldn't hide her amusement but wouldn't be drawn on why.

That left the largest building unoccupied and available as a common area for cooking, meeting, story-telling and working. There was considerable work to be done, though the labour of scribes were subject to work essential for basic survival. As the year moved on, so did many of the birds and especially those that were easily caught. Little by little they were forced to depend quite heavily on the sea and lofty windswept plots for vegetables.

A roster was soon devised that offered two persons minimum to accompany either Owen or Dallan on hunting, fishing or foraging trips. Hunting and fishing spots were strictly regulated to encourage recovery but foraging was more of an adventure for adrenaline junkies. They would scour every inch of Skellig and then start over, following an identical pattern each time. Small treasures from edible seaweeds to shellfish and the occasional driftwood top up, were celebrated with hot herbal teas and tipples of less savoury home brews.

It was on one of these trips that Ignatius, Suivne and Dallan came across a flock of dark penguins like the one that Ignatius had seen on that first fateful day. That lone bird had the company of about thirty others randomly scattered around the lower ledges of Seal Cove. However, what made them different from any penguin he'd previously seen, was the shape of their wide serrated bills.

Using swords as an analogy, if a real penguin's beak was a streamlined and wieldy foil, then these birds were equipped with something closer to a sawn-off claymore. The beaks looked similar to those of puffins but many times larger, and the birds ahead of them sat up on the sea surface like giant ducks, whereas penguins could slide seal-like between water and air.

"What do you call those birds?" He asked the boy softly, using rudimentary but rapidly improving Gaelic.

"They are sometimes called sea-horses?" Said Dallan, his blue eyes flashing this way and then that, taking in every small movement of everything in the immediate environment.

Ignatius thought he'd heard wrong. "Sea-horses? But they don't look anything like horses, do they?"

"But they sound like them when they get excited. Me and Owen used to call them 'Easy Dinner', but that was before that big female arrived and did away with the old Patriarch." He pointed out a particularly anxious looking bird occupying the highest ledge. It appeared to be at least a head taller than the others.

"I think she might have killed him because we haven't seen a sign of him for some time. We called him the old man because he was either senile or forgetful. All we had to do was offer him food and once he'd eaten his share, he'd call out to the others. If we took just one and did that as quietly as we could, he'd have forgotten about it next time we came along.

Big mother up there does the opposite and keeps them all at a distance from us. So we'll just drop a crab bait for now and then see what comes up. One of you will need to keep an eye out for those rogue waves while I'm down there and the other can try the fishing line, OK?"

Danel discouraged Tara from hunting and foraging, though she enjoyed it just as much as the boys and men. She was also quite good at fishing, though it was seldom that any of them caught more than the two boys, who it seemed were bred to survive anywhere. Danel was always the first to fall asleep at night however, usually after the only girl on Skellig made him a brew of warm herbal tea.

Quite soon, it became obvious to anyone with eyes that Tara and Ignatius shared more than just a casual interest in each other, though they did have to be especially discreet around Dooah's two young spies. Falling asleep as early as he did, it was only a matter of time before Danel awoke early enough to discover Satyan sleeping in the spot reserved for Ignatius and so he stopped taking herbal tea. The problem for him however, was that Tara was as ingenious as she was adept at administering potions, so he tended to sleep early regardless.

"My only worry, aside from ensuring that we have enough food and won't die of exposure, is that you could get pregnant." He said from a distance of maybe a centimetre after a particularly intense tryst.

"Do you fear children so much?" She asked. Even in the dark he could see her normally voluminous eyes narrow.

"A child with you would be nothing short of a miracle for me, but you would need to go to Munster to find a midwife and Dooah wouldn't be happy with either of us, nor with Danel." They both laughed at that.

"Dooah doesn't call me Magus for nothing. Even out here on the edge of nowhere, I can find the ingredients to make potions for most things, so don't think of running off with another woman."

Their laughter was sure to carry all the way to the first cell, so they had to cover their mouths to stifle it. "I'll have to get back to my bed and switch places with your brother, so he can get back to his." He whispered at length.

"Fine, but only when you've kept me warm some more." She said, lewdly throwing off an animal skin to further cool her own.

Earlier in the evening they made a game of finding a safe place for her brooch, just in case. They made their way slowly around the cell scanning at her precise eye height and found it in the right hand, sunrise corner. An irregularly shaped stone hid a small crevice, which was too narrow for his hand. It took her long fingers to position the brooch where it could only be recovered by someone who knew it was there.

Everyone on Skellig, with the probable exceptions of Owen and Dallan, had experienced better and possibly luxurious living by comparison, but comfort creates discomfort whereas, nothing trumps survival. Raise a child in a prison and they will acclimatise until they learn of something better beyond the walls. Luxury provides options that are enjoyed on a scale of one to ten or not at all, but simplicity reduces life to what is good and what is not, with nothing in between.

In a spartan essene existence, whatever doesn't make you cry makes you smile and anything that prolongs life is priceless. In that spirit of survival, rain drops sparkling like diamonds are far more precious, because they are also water being collected, filtered and refreshed, ready to drink. Where basic requirements are appreciated for what they really are, discernment and spirituality are also raised to levels as high as Skellig itself.

Suivne started writing short stories of everyday events in their pristine paradise that paradoxically swapped places with purgatory, where nothing happened but hiding from the elements and from life itself. He then worked his way up to poetry and hymns evocative of his and their continuous spiritual awakening.

In Persia, Satyan studied for the Zoroastrian priesthood until he witnessed the other face of its spirit of wisdom, Ahura Mazda. The evangelists of the first monotheistic religion turned out to be quite forceful and violent while spreading their good news in neighbouring Armenia. Satyan was disillusioned and turned to Christianity, which adopted some core elements of Zoroastrianism, such as the virgin birth of a future prophet of major significance. But when he witnessed the atrocities of the Church of Rome for himself, he lost faith in religions generally. Ignatius chose to leave him ignorant of the waves of Islamic and Christian Crusades still to come.

As a 'so called' Priscillian heretic, Danel suffered the loss of his entire community for believing in a less autocratic church than that mandated by Rome, its emperors and popes. Suivne made no secret of his admiration for the Irish heretic Pelagius, which made a heretic of him also and also no friend of Rome.

As a Jesuit, Ignatius took an oath of allegiance to the Pope that included the words "Iustum, necar reges impious", it is just to kill heretic kings and if kings were considered collateral, then why not simpler red blooded heretics. He'd also taken a vow of celibacy and followed that with an oath of allegiance to the pagan king of Munster, which superseded all other oaths and allegiances. It was only when he heard the living testimony of his fellow exiles that he realised he'd been duped by all but a heathen.

By virtue of his undoubted poetic talents, Suivne was given the task of assembling their combined heretical thoughts to produce a common spiritual aspiration. Following established tradition, he proposed that it be written in Latin but not exclusively so. He wanted to exercise poetic license by also using significant words taken from the mother tongues of each of the contributors, along with a more generous smattering of Gaelic, simply because that's where they were.

It was work for foul weather, which was often. But the exercise demanded so much dedicated attention that the purgatory aspect of winter on Skellig was purged. There was no longer such a state as waiting for the sake of waiting.

Christmas interrupted production and Ignatius explained that in his culture, it was the celebration of Yeshua's birth in which gifts were usually exchanged. He didn't tell them that Jesus was most probably born in spring but that was academic, because no-one could be sure when December 25th fell, simply because there was no December. However,

Suivne was reasonably sure when the winter solstice arrived, despite the fact that the sun hadn't shown for a week. Nevertheless, Ignatius added four nominal days and declared the first Christmas on Skellig, which called for another, special mass.

With no gifts to exchange, yet another night of storytelling was arranged and this one with a real Christian and Yeshua theme. It was an herbal tea and dubious brew evening, which was far from a routine event, but which inevitably went on far too late. Tara got bored when the jokes became bawdy and she rose to leave not long after the two young boys. Under strict instructions to monitor the straits from dawn to dusk at least, they couldn't risk sleeping late.

"Are you forgetting something, Magus?" Asked Danel quietly.

"I don't think so." She said with a smile but also a raised eyebrow because only Dooah called her 'Magus".

"Your escort?"

"Oh, I've heard this story many times before and my brother is not even halfway through it and he's not going to let his sister interrupt it."

"Not that escort." She was Magus because she could do otherwise inexplicable things, yet no-one expected someone with the tone and demeanour of a Persian Princess to blush.

When they sputtered, coughed and laughed their way to a semblance of silence, Danel shrugged. "I'm so tired of people stepping over, or more often on me when I'm trying to sleep. It's like there are twice as many people sleeping inside and no-one needs to piss that often."

"What about Dooah?" Ignatius asked as he passed Danel and took Tara's hand in his.

"The King gambled and lost, but I doubt he'll hold my daughter responsible for that and besides … leaving a woman as beautiful as Tara here is like putting a fox in the same pen as the geese."

Without pausing for breath, he looked at Satyan. "As her brother however, I did expect you to play a better part in keeping her safe."

It appeared that Satyan had a statement preprepared. "I'm her brother Danel, not her father and surely the best way to protect my sister is to let her have another protector of her own choice. Anyway, I know my sister and she was never likely to be easily seduced by anything or anyone. In fact, it's been my experience that she is more of a manipulator than manipulated." Satyan laughed along with the others as they applauded his vastly improved latin and his Jesuit teacher took a bow.

When they quieted down, Ignatius cautioned. "But we still need to keep this from Dooah's two boys."

“I’m not sure they’re old enough to care about such things.” Suivne put in.

“They are young but they are still spies and besides, I’d prefer to tell Dooah myself whenever he gets around to calling me ashore.” Said Ignatius and they left for bed together for the first time.

“Happy Christmas.” Shouted Danel, Suivne and Satyan after them.

A prolonged wet and cold spell followed in which the entire rock was covered in oppressive layers of dank cloud for more than a fortnight. At the onset of winter, such dour and restrictive conditions would have sapped their spirits and left them close to despair but in the case of Ignatius in particular, it afforded him even more time for the loves of his life.

Despite his best intentions, his whispered sweet nothings did include accounts of people flying through the sky and leaving white contrails behind them as markers. Tara was intrigued to discover that people could actually witness events as they occurred and in every corner of the world, while drinking morning tea. In return, she mesmerised him with detailed descriptions of lives lived in exotic paradises, on endless migrations and in races against constantly rising interglacial seas.

An enchanting, almost immortal temptress, never born in the same place twice was far too valuable a gift for any heretic priest but he accepted her in full knowledge that such things were never meant to last.

Ignatius had lost nearly all of the religious and clerical baggage that he was trained for so long to retain and expound. He also assumed some unusual lay slash secular privilege with responsibility, but he still considered himself a Jesuit inside, be that of the severely flawed or much enhanced variety. So what remained of his non-survival activity time that wasn't spent with Tara, was devoted to perfecting his prayer and to the completion of their joint literary masterpiece. The latter was already a virtual thesis on the essence of spirituality, presented in hybrid latin verse.

Since he was the major contributor and with the finishing line in sight, Ignatius was offered the honour of providing a title. There are few secrets between lovers and as it happened, he was also looking for an appropriate way to mark Tara's birthday just two days later. So he recalled the king's compulsion to climb the southern peak and give thanks for what he was given, and then ask for inspiration to handle whatever might lie ahead.

According to his calendar, it was another Thursday outside. Not that the name of the day mattered, except that it identified the following day as one of full fasting for followers of the old religion. So he thought it appropriate to also spend Aoine in meditation and prayer up there and despite the recent rain. Following the example set by royalty however, was easier said than done. The climb was so literally breathtaking, dizzying, tortuous and treacherous that when he eventually reached the last flat parapet, his first prayer was for a safe descent and the second, to ease the trembling in his limbs.

Suivne was an artist but he also wrote well because he was an avid reader. He ingested, regurgitated and then digested every line of what he possessed of the old and new testaments. Those were his treasures and he kept them locked away in a solid, polished and ancient leather folder. Ignatius was only lately permitted to touch them and it came as a genuine shock that a primitive monk could be so well versed in scripture, while he himself, a Jesuit Teacher-Priest was an expert on nothing more than dogma.

Sitting on that tiny terrace where only Munster's god anointed kings had sat before, brought him yet another minor revelation. Suivne said it was King Solomon who wrote 'Ecclesiastes' and two lines were now etched in his heretic psyche.

"He has made everything beautiful in its time. He has also set eternity in the human heart; yet no one can fathom what God has done from beginning to end."

So, since God is nothing if not all things to all men, he sat alone and aloft and simply radiated gratitude to the same awesome presence that Dooah could sense surrounding Skellig. That act could be laughable to a casual observer, to whom Ignatius would appear to have absolutely nothing to be grateful for. But he enjoyed the recently acquired insight that nothing obscured nothing. Each physical possession blocks whatever lies behind it and even glass blocks the wind. He could never see everything, but he could see more than most, especially what was important and in that regard, he had so much to be eternally grateful for.

Top of his list was the extremely unlikely circumstances of Tara and himself together on Skellig, or anywhere for that matter. It was nothing short of scooping the biggest ever prize in a universal lottery. He readily acknowledged the implied terms and conditions and simply requested that the relationship might end later rather than sooner.

He did so in the belief that it was something to be selected from the infinite possibilities within himself, which then made it so. It was also a fact that their closely knit group continued to be protected, even after Dooah's departure. Lastly, he gave thanks for keeping the rain at bay while he searched for title worthy of their communal work and for a little more time to put the polish on a gift worthy of a Magus.

The thing was, if Dooah was wrong about any aspects of God or of gods being projected from or into Skellig, it didn't matter. That was because Dooah also had infinity in his heart and if he believed in something so sincerely, then it was also a fact to be taken from his limitless possibilities.

Ignatius had moved far beyond religious incantations requiring bells, incense and church organs measured in tons to give them gravitas. He knew that God was light and life because it said so in the bible and because he had infinity in his heart, then it was fact for him. What was truly fathomless, was the number of faces that God could present to be seen by everyone everywhere.

However, Ignatius got a shock in return. He couldn't have anticipated the sense of foreboding that fell like a shadow over his spirit. It was the discordant merging of his rising aspiration dampened by despair on descent and he realised there was simply no hope of reaching the highs of previous spiritual communions. Eventually, it became so unsettling that he struggled to stay focussed on his last two tasks. It was only through stoic perseverance, applied in the spirit and discipline of a Zen Buddhist Monk, that morning became evening and he felt a soft rain. It was that gentle shower that supplied all the inspiration he needed, though he also cursed it when he slipped more than once on the climb back down.

The title ‘Revelatio Pluvit', or ‘Revelation Rains’ was enthusiastically endorsed by his co-authors and most eagerly by Suivne, who waxed lyrical about its many analogous possibilities. The simple act of five very distinct minds in such complete accord, produced something purer than happiness that he couldn’t then contaminate with his unease.

However, Tara was also highly attuned to Skellig, though in ways he could never understand.

She'd set out early with Dallan and Owen as her eager students. They descended to the saddle shaped plateau between the two peaks, where three routes onward to the multiple choice of landing or embarkation points diverged. She aimed to replenish her herb, guano and God only knew what else she planned to add to her collection.

"Something is wrong." She said, when he found her waiting in her cell and he became concerned to find her shivering when he embraced her.

"I thought it could be different but it's like Scelec Tearmann has finished with me early." She said shuddering.

"With us, you mean, though I think I sensed something might not be right." He had to agree, only slightly puzzled by the exclusion of everyone else from her ominous insight. All he could think of doing just then was holding her tighter for longer.

Her birthday was unusually mild with barely a breeze but it was also quite humid. From the vantage point of the four beehive huts, thin clouds of mist moved beneath them and then through the two peaks from the Atlantic side. Beams from a sallow slanted sun illuminated the island obliquely in small select patches. These roved lazily from one side to the other creating the illusion of Skellig floating above the sea. Struggling to see through the bright fluffy clouds tumbling off Skellig towards Munster, two sets of keen eyes watched for signs of a long overdue boat.

It was the first sign of winter being forced to acknowledge the approach of spring and it lifted the oppressive melancholy of the previous evening, when they didn't make love but just lay there together. He spent the night weighing the end of their spartan honeymoon against divorce and her impending forced remarriage to Crochur Dairinne. Her thoughts were somehow worse by the look on her face when her special day dawned.

So, he eased out a ring in an attempt to cheer her up. It was crafted by each of them in their own special way. Danel supplied the link, which was once heavy enough to hold his scabbard to his belt in battle. Suivne filed the rough pieces out of it and then artfully inscribed her name, her age and the date after AD, Anno Domini. The only problem was writing the year in its latin form, because it filled more than half of the ring. Satyan then spent hours resizing it to fit her finger, once Ignatius provided the internal circumference in cord, stealthily taken while she slept. Ignatius then polished it until his fingers turned blue and the bronze took on a reasonable shade of gold.

What happened next stunned him. She shuddered, then cried and handed it back.

"Why?"

Owen began shouting one word over and over again. “Cashel, Cashel, Cashel.”

The boy was quite agitated but there would be time for that later. “Why?” he asked again but with a whine that sounded like pleading.

“I’ve got it wrong. I can’t believe I’ve got it wrong.” She started backing away.

“Cashel, Cashel. Is marav eiy Dooah.” Dallan was pulling at what was left of his sleeve, demanding his attention. Then it sank in. Dooah was dead. He had to squint for a while, but with the help of the boy’s steady finger he counted six … no eight boats making slow but measurable progress towards them while cutting across the breeze.

“Cinnte?” He asked. Maybe it was a mistake. Maybe they were from Ventry.

“Cinnte.” Said the boy who apparently had his instructions. He and his cousin sprung into action by grabbing hold of Tara. They began dragging her out of the compound and then pushed her ahead of them. Soon they were into the narrowest part of the pathway and Ignatius had to be careful as he pushed through the boys to join her.

Their small boat stuck into a sheltered ledge above the rocks was no secret. The boys would use it to rescue their uncle’s queen from Cashel.

“Wait.” He said in Latin and then again in Gaelic, but they kept pushing her along at a relentless pace. So he was obliged to insinuate himself between them and her when she had trouble keeping her feet.

“What did you get wrong?” He threw the question at her.

“We must have lost a day somewhere, Ignatius.” She risked a worried glance at him. “Now just go and hide somewhere or surrender yourself.”

She then started running with the boys away from him, further downhill … and she was right, he thought. They couldn’t hope to defend her from so many.

“Let me help you.” He shouted and started down once more.

“No.” She screamed. “I never wake for my twenty-second birthday. It doesn’t matter now. I loved …”

Like him, she made the mistake of looking back at the wrong time and went head over heels down the hill like a discarded rag doll. The two fleet-footed boys stayed in hot pursuit, but they couldn’t get a physical hold on her while also keeping their own feet under them.

Then she went over the edge after rolling over a narrow section of tough grass. It happened almost serenely and without a sound, which was impossible in itself.

However, he knew Skellig well and she'd fallen just short of the actual cliff face. He persuaded himself that she'd be OK provided she was able to stop herself from tumbling and could grab hold of something but the clumps of grass quickly petered out and in any case, they weren't anchored very well. The three of them went over the crest and quickly out of view, so he launched himself carelessly after them.

"TARA!. DALLAN! OWEN!" He shouted in turn and had great difficulty stopping himself from overshooting the critical point but there was nothing there. A thick patch of fog, made thicker by being caught stagnant in the curve of cliff wall, completely blocked his view beyond maybe five metres. But it wasn't just a visual thing, it was suddenly far too quiet, not even the birds …

"TARA! ANSWER ME."

After a while you don't hear the birds on Skellig. Their cacophonous chaos becomes part of the background, like breathing at night. Just then however, each shrill call returned from the absolute silence, just mocked him.

"Oh my God."

Then louder. "OH MY GOD."

Then he screamed. "WHAT DID I EVER DO TO YOU … WHAT?"

To his right a movement … taking shape like adding flesh to a spectre until it was big enough to be an adult.

“Thank God.” He muttered, oblivious to his hypocrisy.

“Hey Roy. There’s a dude up here who thinks he’s Chewbacca or sumpin'.” Then more shadows materialised from the mist until they made a group of four, but the really frightening thing about them was their use of English.

“English??” He was stunned, but they weren’t surprised in the least.

“Naw. We’re from the studio, lookin’ to do a sequel … Hollywood.” He was a tall man and only a shade or two lighter than Brother Chaz.

“How did you get here? We had to apply for special permits from the Irish Government to get in and out before the tourist season starts. They said we’d have the place pretty much to ourselves.” When Ignatius couldn’t speak, they accepted his reticence as a possible language problem.

“I’m Steve by the way … and this is the producer, Roy Knowles … JJ won’t be on this trip.”

“Jeez Steve.” Roy cut in as he hauled himself up the last few steps.

“Dude looks like he’s been here a while … what with all the Chewbacca skins and that wild-man beard goin’ on. You OK Man? You lose something here?”

A smaller wiry man squeezed through the group and pushed his face so close to the priest's that they shared the smell of exhaled bacon, egg and pork sausage.

"It's you. You're the priest who dived into Seal Cove. Jayzus … They put you down as dead." He grew an instant smile but then lost it just as quickly.

Jimmy Maguire wanted to smack him there and then, though not for being on Skellig pre-season and without a permit. He wanted payback for hours spent under serious interrogation in Portmagee. Sergeant high and mighty McSweeney had convinced himself there'd been a murder, and he still looked at him funny whenever their path's crossed.

But as angry as he was, Jimmy couldn't hit a crying man and especially not a Jesuit priest who just then dropped to his knees, sobbing like some crazy kid who'd just lost a favourite toy.

16 - SQUARE PLUGS

- Valencia Lifeboat - Comms Log -
- January 13th -
- 11:05 -

A VHF radio erupts into sound like someone is pulling the antenna off, and then sticks it back in again.

“So, you know what I’m going to say. Where and what? Over.”

“It’s not a major disaster, Sean. Looks like minimum crew over to Skellig and back, just to blow the cobwebs off, but we’ll have to be fast. Over”

“Not a bother. We can be away by midday but I’ll need more information. Over”

“Roger that, Valencia. They tell me there’s some lunatic needs to be brought back from the monastery on Skellig and from all accounts, he seems to have been there quite a while. The only thing is, it means sending over the mountain rescue team as well. I’ve got Squib on the blower and he says there’ll be himself plus two, including a paramedic. Over.”

“Copy that, but I’d have thought there were warmer places to see in the New Year. I’m assuming he’s a him? Over.”

“Affirm, Valencia. One adult male so far, but they’re looking into reports of an adult female and two boys also. Bad enough taking yourself out there, but what kind of nut job brings a young family camping on Skellig at this time of year? Over.”

“Roger and then Roger again … anyway, … Ok. So, all told that we’ll have seven souls over and hopefully eight but possibly eleven coming back. Seas are flat calm down here so don’t worry about seats. Two of the lads can stand, but we might need two trips if everyone shows up. Any chance of a Helo to speed things up? He has to be suffering from exposure at the very least and Kerry sunset is 16:15 -ish. Over.”

“They can’t confirm a chopper until later, Valencia. Seems cloud cover’s a problem right now, but they’re not saying they can’t send it later, when the clouds lift a bit. Maybe for the that second trip if it’s still on. Over.”

“That’s well copied, though we can’t see Skellig from the boat to give you an update on the weather, but I’ll be sure to send a report when we arrive on station. Over.”

“Ok, Valencia … and standby one for an update just in.”

“Valencia standing by …”

More crackles, then silence, then louder crackles with heavy breathing and a clunk like someone just dropped the handset.

"Seems it's the priest who committed suicide last year."

"Valencia here. Say again. Over."

"It's the Jesuit who tried to kill himself last year, after all that trouble in his family. Over."

"Oh Yeah … Moloney. I remember. We must have covered two thousand square miles of sea lookin' for his body and he wasn't even dead. The environmentalists will go nuts … anyway, let me get busy prepping the boat and finishing the callout. I'll set ETD at Twelve Midday to maximise daylight. Ok with you? Over."

"Sounds good … and Valencia, you still there?"

"Valencia here, go ahead."

"Make that plus one more out and back, a specialist trauma doctor or something, details for the manifest will follow by email. Over."

"Another quack? We could be in trouble if the woman and two boys materialise. This is a nice boat but it's not exactly a cruise ship y'know. Over."

"Yeah, yeah. I don't know why they need a second opinion today when the priority should be on getting casualties out. I'm guessing they know more than they're saying about the injuries or the other casualties. Anyway … it doesn't matter to us does it … we just do as we're told? Over."

“Got that right. Valencia is over and out.”

Mountain Rescue Team -13th January 13:10.

‘Contact with film crew on the saddle of Skellig Michael. One Steve Hall brought us to the third beehive reading left to right. Inside, one semi-responsive adult male found wearing animal skins over what used to be an anorak. Hasn’t seen a razor for some time but sitting upright. Paramedic and doctor left in attendance.’

“So. Did you ask the film crew if they brought him up here or if he was able to walk here by himself, as in, unaided?” Said without looking at either of the mountain rescue team paramedic or their apparently catatonic patient, while also digging into a bag of considerable proportions and then laying out a selection of soft plastic packages sealed with water-proof zip-locks.

“No.” He answered, trying to catch a better view of the rather slight owner of the calm but fragile sounding female voice emanating from the depths of an oversized orange hood.

“Are you going to?” It was a question from the same mysterious source and it held neither rancour nor humour.

“I suppose.” Said the paramedic setting down his comparatively puny bag of bare essentials.

Fortunately for him, Steve had stayed behind and was chatting to Squib, so he was quickly back inside again. "Well. They say they just followed him up here from about halfway down to the camping area that we passed on the way up. Apparently, he's been pretty much as you see him since morning."

Smatterings of a discussion outside the beehive could be overheard quite easily. She heard the name Tara being mentioned and someone being sent to search for signs of a recent campfire and two young boys.

The paramedic went on. "The Office of Public Works foreman positively ID'd him as the priest that went missing last year."

Just then, she pulled down the oversized hood of the all-weather one-piece that had to be zipped almost up to her forehead. On the trip over, she'd kept her head down as they do, playing with either a phone or a tablet, so it was hard to get a good look at the doctor but just then, he almost fell over backwards.

"You sure you're qualified?"

Jonathan Healy was accustomed to working either alone or with a designated colleague. Doctors didn't usually get their shoes dirty until casualties were handed over with their assessments. What was happening here was not just an unwelcome precedent. He didn't like the feeling of being redundant, especially to a doctor so young. This one looked like she'd barely finished college.

"Cora Quinn … and this is my ID, Mr. … Healy." She said curtly, pausing very briefly to get some detail from his.

What struck him then was all the letters after her name. "Sorry Doc. It's just that … well… I …"

"Never mind, Mr. Healy. How long do you estimate it will take you and your team to get him back down to the lifeboat?"

"Well, that will depend on what you can do for him, Doc. He looks pretty out of it to me. You saw the stretcher, but if we need to use it then were talking three maybe four hours, though I'll need to confirm that with Squib."

"Ok then. We're not going anywhere for awhile."

He turned with a grunt of disgust and a clearly heard muttering of "Holy Shit," when he realised he'd just been dismissed. Outside, he caught up with Squib, so called because he would never be the life or soul of any party.

"Mary Poppins in there wants to know how long it will take us to get him down to the lifeboat." He wasn't quite sure he was out of earshot but he didn't care, and followed that with. "What a witch!"

Squib didn't seem to notice the insult and looked at his watch again. The lifeboat Bosun had really laid into him for turning up only five minutes late and then gave him a rollicking about sunset and some non-existent helicopter. The guy had to be on something but nevertheless, he calculated three hours if the rain held off, which was looking increasingly likely.

"Three hours if we're lucky." Jonathan relayed to the Doctor, who had unzipped the overall down to reveal a very nubile figure from her slim waist upwards and his mouth hung open.

"Thank you Mr. Healy." Being called a witch wasn't new to her, so she did what she usually did and pretended she hadn't heard it.

"Jonny. Everyone calls me Jonny."

"… OK Jonny. Why don't we take the element of luck out of those three hours with you and your team leaving me here alone to do what I do best. That way, you can get yourselves and your gear ready to walk him down in say an hour. That will give me time to put some go-go juice into him and we can save an hour at least … but I just need space. This hut thing is very cramped and I need to fit an 'IntraV' and also take his vitals from time to time while the drip does its work."

"Well, that will be great. A walk-down would be an excellent result for us … super. Though maybe I should stay here to assist you? What will I call you by the way?"

“Doctor will be fine.”

“Sure … Doc. I’ll leave you to it then.”

Anticipating another tantrum, Cora smiled sweetly. “Thanks for the offer Jonny, but I have a routine I like to follow, but I’ll be sure to call you if anything changes.” That seemed to take some of the sting out of it, but he nevertheless backed away more disappointed than merely useless.

Inside, the young doctor brought her face closer to his, so she could clearly see his eye movements. He wasn’t looking at her, so she spoke clearly and with some intensity. “This might seem a little rushed right now and to be honest, I haven't had much time to prepare a speech for you. You see, despite what you might think, this isn’t easy for me either.” He still wasn’t looking, which meant he wasn’t listening either.

“You have no idea how hard it is to stay sane as a kid while dead people’s memories seep into your conscience, not to mention the small detail that they’re all earlier versions of yourself … speaking in tongues … and with none of them more than twenty-one years old. DO YOU?” He flinched but that was all he did.

“Dammit.” Too loud, she thought but also too late.

“You OK Doc?”

“Sure Jonny. Just trying to get a response to audio … you know?

“I’ll be just outside then.”

“Thanks Jonny.”

She could hear them talking outside and she knew that the topic had changed and that she was the subject. Boys and men tended to do that when they saw her for the first time and expected something else, like a leggy blonde, or maybe a brunette.

Hair as red as hers was despised more often than it was tolerated, and it wasn’t usually about the hair at all. It was the pasty white skin that comes with it. Her legs were good but even better when also kept secret.

But she’d got the priest’s attention. He was looking a bit dazed but he was looking, which was something.

“Ok then. Let’s get this done.” She said, taking a deep breath and keeping a wary eye towards the door.

“I could have come here years ago or even last year. I mean, being born and raised so close to where one of us once lived is like an omen, but I couldn’t put it off any longer. Besides, I wasn’t sure which beehive it was. You see, I can’t remember every little detail, just the big things like falling in and out of love and the endless ‘almost’ dying.”

Ignatius just looked at her blankly as she rabitted on with superfluous nonchalance. “Thankfully, that tends to bring the curtain down on one of us and there’s nothing after that. We never get to be twenty-two but then, we don’t actually sign off either. We come uncomfortably close, but not that close.” She could tell by the way his irises were contracting and expanding that was surfacing, though how much of what she was saying was being understood, was something else.

So she forged ahead with words prepared only an hour in advance. “I’m not Tara and I never expected to meet you, so I don’t love you but I do know you. In fact … I know you much better than your own Mammy does, … I mean did. Anyway, I also know that Tara loved you. She … we … we’re like sisters but even closer. Tara was a bit of a nut job though, and she made it far too easy for you to love her, but she did love you back, right up to the end. She really shouldn’t have done that. Do you know what I’m trying to say?

“Tara’s sister?” It was whispered in disbelief.

“Yeah. I’m more than that but the thing is, as I understand it, you probably loved her only this morning and that has to be hard on you, but I never got to know you like that at all and never thought I would … not really. You see, none of us has reached twenty-two, except me, today. That’s why I took such a big chance today … and everything.” He frowned an all encompassing frown.

“Don’t worry about it too much for now. It’ll make sense later.” She said and then walked to the back of the cell, talking as she went.

“Like I said, I only remember important stuff and there seems to be a lot more to this place than when you and Tara hid the brooch, so you need to point me in the right direction, OK?

“Sure.” He said, totally bemused by most of what she was saying, though more and more of it was falling on fertile ground and some very strange possibilities were sprouting in some very dark corners.

“Is it over there?” The girl with luminous fairy green eyes and great shocks of long red hair was shaking him with one hand and pointing with the other.

“You need to help me out here … Father Moloney.” Calling him by that unfamiliar and unwanted name seemed to jump-start something inside him.

“What do you want here …?”

“I’m looking for something. But I’m not sure I’m looking in the right place?”

The mist slowly rising from Skellig outside was doing the same inside also. “How could she possibly know about the brooch?” He thought.

“There’s nothing there for you.” He said dourly. The english words felt awkward and very foreign. He was beyond tired and felt more like the walking dead and she’d said something about him walking down to a boat. She had to be joking. He was there until they dragged him away kicking and screaming.

“This is where you and Tara slept, right?”

“Tara? Yes. Tara … here…” He was on his feet but a swarm of shooting stars almost blinded him when his blood caught inertia and failed to keep pace with his intentions, so he fell towards her. This caused the drip to detach but he was oblivious to that. The girl was a lot stronger than she looked and he wasn’t up to doing much more than falling, so she just guided him down again to reset the IntraV.

“We need to get the brooch, Ignatius. Please stay with me.”

He was incensed. It was Tara’s brooch and if she couldn’t have it then he’d put it in a museum as a sort of showcased original but ‘Alternate’ Tara Brooch. Strange he thought, how that name Tara was also an old Persian name, but it seemed he’d muttered some part of that out loud.

“Yeah, I know.” She said drily and then followed that with, “Aahh the funny shaped head-high stone. Here it is.”

She played her fingers deftly into a crevice behind a stone with holes in it that gave it a comic yet ghostly face and then beamed when her fingers made contact. Then she extracted it ever so slowly, like an inflamed appendix that might be seeping and you simply can't risk dropping something like that back where it came from.

He was still a little woozy, but also very irate. "It's an ancient artefact and it belongs in a museum. In fact, it's a crime to remove anything from Skellig." He made an effort to snatch it away, but she was as fast as she was simply surprising.

"Let's get this straight, Father. This is my brooch because I fully intended to do what was asked of me by a king to earn it and deep down, you knew she had no choice about that. The thing is, you never really know that you're not going to live to be twenty-two until you don't. Because of you, Tara lived more in hope than the rest of us but if it keeps you happy, we can consider this my birthday present from me to myself."

He took his time appraising her, as if seeing her for the first time and if he was totally honest, he'd have to say that she looked barely twenty, until those green eyes caught hold of his. Then she looked anything from challenging to extraordinarily brash and maybe just a little too feisty to ever be genuinely serious about anything except herself.

"You'd have to be top of your class in everything from age twelve onwards to have any chance of qualifying as a doctor by age twenty-two." He knew what he was talking about because that's how long it took him to become a Jesuit, even though he started later.

"You're so right, Father Ignatius. But I've gotten used to being called exemplary in the study department since I was ten but then, you know that Tara was way ahead of her time and that was just her. You could say that medicine runs in the family. Also, when you're 99% sure that you're going to die aged twenty-one, but can't tell anyone because they'd lock you up for sure, then what else is there to do except be a good girl, work hard and stay quiet. Here, eat this."

She passed him a bar of chocolate covered toffee crisp and then one of those tiny cans of cola that you get as a mixer. He nearly had an orgasm when the sugar rush almost caught up with the flavour only to be pipped at the post.

Half an hour later they were climbing down from the monastery with Squib leading the way and Ryan just behind the priest and holding the rope that held him taught. Jonny was literally holding his hand with Doctor Cora Quinn bringing up the rear. They passed the expanding encampment of overly colourful tents and when Ignatius made eye contact with Steve they exchanged small waves, one of acknowledgment and thanks and the other a well-wish.

Cora Quinn continued talking like they were still alone in the cell, which Ignatius found disconcerting, but that meant that his brain was getting closer to being back where he needed it to be.

"I told you the complex is much bigger now than when we first shared it, what with the monastery, the oratory and all. It was lucky for me that you just wandered back into the same beehive that we shared back then but then, this seems to be my really lucky day." She was right about that.

He'd simply sleepwalked back to the only connection he had with Tara. He didn't even see all the 'later' constructions. It was something like the day he'd arrived on Skellig but in reverse, with too many mysteries and a stunning, if overly talkative flame haired girl who looked nothing like Tara, but who was also no stranger to their time together.

It was also irritating the way she could break long concentrated silences with unexpected bursts of noisy irrelevant chat. "I should tell you now, so there's no misunderstanding later, that I've been with others. That means that I haven't been pining away for you like you might think I should have been. Put another way, I had plenty of other options to exercise today, but I'm here on Skellig only to reclaim what's mine." Squib looked past Jonny to Ryan, glancing at Cora as he did, but said nothing.

"I will have to admit though, that it really is a magic place and definitely somewhere for firsts, even if that's a priest falling out of love with God and into bed with a beautiful young dark girl. It does have an ambience that the naive might find very disarming, so I'm sure no-one can blame you for that." Her laugh was forced and came out more like a cackle.

Ignatius was starting to feel quite good, physically at least, though mentally he was worried by how liberal her tongue was with a situation she could never hope to understand.

"There's been others?" He threw it out straight ahead knowing some of it would blow back to her. He also wanted to get her off the thorny subject of a relationship that he considered holy, in every sense.

"You better believe it, Father. Your special friend Tara was really something, but she was also too soft. She was a waste of beauty and brains who also broke the rules. The sisterhood nowadays has to be tougher and more streetwise, but we've also got standards. None of us would intentionally break any boy's heart."

Her pause was timed to perfection, like a performer with an audience hanging on her every word while feigning indifference.

"Growing up with the virtual guarantee of not having a twenty-second birthday to share with the same boyfriend you shared your bed with after your twenty-first, tends to put a damper on commitment and stuff. I don't expect you to admit it, but men are just as fragile as they think women are and there'd be so many tears. I mean, just look at yourself. You're a mess and yet when you really think about it, nothing has actually been lost. Someone who was born in prehistory died young and it probably happened a lot back then, but you're still with us." It was true but it also stung and he stopped in his tracks, which caused Ryan to almost bump into his back.

"You OK?" But Ignatius just turned around to glare past Ryan at Cora.

If a part of Tara really lived on in this attention seeker, then he was looking at a very small part though she did have a point. It was thanks to her treatment and his improving state of mind that he was able to see something else as well. He could see that Cora wasn't even a reflection of the real thing.

"But this is the first time I've ever been twenty-two, and I mean ever. Now I can live with the confidence of having a future, where attachments can last … if I want them to."

Ryan started shaking his head slowly from side to side, unsure if he wanted to hear more but doing nothing to interrupt her, while Ignatius decided not to get drawn in. This resulted in the conversation string pretty much expiring, until Squib decided to belatedly chip in. "You two must have known each other pretty well?"

Cora Quinn's use of instant come-backs cum put-downs were good enough for the stage, and they also served the purpose of showing that she was not someone to be toyed with. She would never be a soft or easy conquest like Tara. "Oh yeah. The Padre and I were quite the couple in a previous life, but he moved on while I stayed stuck in the past. In fact, we might have met right here on Skellig at about the same time as St. Patrick was doing his thing, you know, driving out snakes and other undesirables."

"Huh." Grunted Squib. It had taken him some minutes to dig deep, find the courage to join the conversation, and then hopefully make a better impression on the young doctor, but there was no way he could follow that.

Ignatius practically skipped off the last step and threw a healthy guffaw down the pathway to his left. There was a boat lying some distance out from where he knew the small quay should be.

"Ahhh. Romeo, Romeo. Good to see that you're well on the road to a full recovery. It must be nice to be deaf to ghosts who still love you." He thought that was uncalled for and added 'nasty' to her growing list of detractions.

He knew he should have stayed quiet but she'd asked for it. "Yes, Doctor Quinn."

He turned to face her. "I'm feeling much better thanks to the brave mountain rescue boys here and to the Valencia Lifeboat people and most especially to you, even more than to God himself …" His ears caught the echo from the rock behind her and he couldn't believe that he sounded almost as bitchy as she had and immediately followed with, "- sorry. I shouldn't have said that."

She heard him, but they were off the slopes and almost where they needed to be. It wasn't a good time to talk while the team coiled their ropes, stashed gloves in pockets and unzipped more zips. They were soon away down the pathway and as they turned the corner he saw the lifeboat about twenty metres off-shore. They'd lowered an inflatable to get in to the small quay and it was just a matter of a short climb down, though wearing a life jacket three times too big.

Jack McGrath was hanging over the lifeboat rails as they approached. The rescue team were left behind to repack their equipment for stowage. So, it was Ignatius first, then Cora and lastly Jonny. A flurry of strong hands and warm smiles welcomed them and then helped them onto the narrow deck.

"Skipper is very happy with the time you boys made." He was talking to Jonathan. "It looks like we all owe each other a pint later. You can sit or stand wherever you want Jonny Boy and well done to all … but you, Father Moloney will have to sit inside … with the nice doctor."

She looked very different with her hood thrown back. The Bosun remembered her as being practically invisible inside her orange suit on the trip out.

"The very nice doctor." He repeated and she smiled a genuine smile while the youngest of his crew led her and her patient along the rails to the door at the back of the main cabin

The Skipper's seat was mounted on a swivel and it was turned backwards, facing into the cabin so he could interact with his crew. He nodded when he got a hand signal through the side window from his second-in-command and then pointed to two seats facing each other on the left as they entered.

Ignatius was struck by the unexpected clutter of radio equipment and storage boxes, but the deckhand was very helpful and studiously guided him to his seat by the elbow. Doctor Cora Quinn surprised no-one when she waved the young man away to sit silently facing Ignatius.

The Skipper was at his side and nodded at Cora, who flashed another very sweet smile. "We need to be very clear on this, Father." He said, speaking louder than he normally would. "They've found no signs of a campfire nor of anyone else up there but you. So I have to ask you if anyone else was lost or went missing out here today?"

Ignatius waited an inordinately long time before answering. "Not today, Captain … and thank you for coming out to collect me. I'm sorry for being such a nuisance." The Captain just nodded.

"And you doctor. Do you have any reason to think that the Reverend Father might be incapable of telling us what really happened up there?"

Cora Quinn showed them a set of perfect teeth. "He's in surprisingly good health Captain and having spoken to him at length, I don't doubt him." Then, a third smile in very quick succession told Ignatius that maybe she was going to try being human for a change.

"Then you are most welcome on board." The Skipper returned to his seat and swung it around to face his console and almost immediately, the radio crackled unintelligibly. Meanwhile, the inflatable returned to collect the mountain rescue team.

Through the opposite window, another boat could be seen joining the one he'd seen earlier. No doubt waiting for the rescue to conclude so they could deliver supplies or whatever to the film crew. He surprised himself by feeling jealous of them, despite the tragedy of losing Tara there.

"So you're still thanking God?" The younger crewman sitting on the opposite side of the cabin seemed preoccupied and totally uninterested in the young doctor's question. Ignatius couldn't help thinking that in truth, the young man was actually shy and deliberately facing away. He however, was also regretting his momentary loss of self-control but nonetheless pleased to see that it might have served some purpose. It did appear that a truce had been declared.

However, judging by her serious expression, she wasn't just asking an idle question.

He once again took in her almost albino features and for a young woman, she appeared to be surprisingly brazen and easily held his gaze. He'd always been something of a loser with women or rather, with girls back in the day and this one reminded him why. If he could somehow put Tara in the Doctor's place he'd probably have to conclude that she was nothing like the lady he felt he'd lost.

She would likely be a product of the new age and just as brash and arrogant as the attractive, pale but overly dour girl facing him. Cora might well be a highly evolved upgrade of the woman he fell in love with, but that would paradoxically make her incompatible with the highly spiritual creature that Tara really was.

Her eyebrows went up when those huge eyes of hers detected a change in the hard configuration of a face that was mostly beard. "You can smile." She teased.

If thoughts of Tara could bring a smile to his face only hours after losing her, then he'd already made great progress. It did unsettle him to acknowledge that it was due in no small part to the lady, no … despite her qualifications, he was looking at a girl over the table, but she still deserved his best answer to her first question.

"Deep down, I'm still a Jesuit, Cora. A different and maybe liberal kind of Jesuit admittedly, but one who pledged to destroy heretic kings wherever they are. The only difference is that they're not where I was told to look."

"Wow. So where are you going to find one of those in these enlightened times?" She was just unstoppable with the banter and he decided to accept the unstated terms of her truce by trying to match her nonchalant enthusiasm.

"Well, I've been on Skellig long enough to reflect on many important things and one of those is that heretics are as common as hypocrites and that would place them everywhere. Heretics led me to believe that their kind were all extinct but that was only so I'd stop looking for them. Now my mission is to confront them and ultimately that will probably take me to Rome, though it's more likely I'll end up in jail or worse along the way."

Her smile was once again unusual in being natural and warm. She was completely transformed and he had to remind himself that Skellig couldn't have been easy for her either. She had just revisited the precise place where such an important aspect of her died. Closer than sisters she said.

"So, that would have to make you something of an upgrade of your old self?" She stunned him with an observation that so closely paralleled his own. But it obliged him to measure just how improved he might really be before responding.

He was maybe the only Jesuit to truly appreciate that God has more than just one face to show. He was trained never to question his training, but discovered that a closed mind only prolongs ignorance. He was ordered to be disciplined but only in dogma and he was told that his celibacy was a sacrifice when it was just a cost cutting exercise. Priests with no baggage were cheaper and you could get more for your buck. Following the original Christian example, he knew that in order to be a real priest, only the unselfish offering of himself would be acceptable, just like Yeshua's. So, yes, all things considered, he was undeniably an upgrade.

And so he agreed with her. "Yes, at least I hope so," He replied softly, "- but since we Jesuits have taken the same vow to expose heretics, it will come down to the real definition of what a heretic truly is. So, I'll probably cut my teeth on a lower ranked Jesuit like the Governor General of the Jesuit Society, before tackling HQ in Rome."

That didn't bring the smile he expected but it did quieten her down for a minute, though it was obvious she was mulling over the implications. "I think you're very naive to think you can fix anything after all this time?"

"I won't try to fix all of it but some of it will be a start, I guess." He responded immediately and then decided to show her how determined he was.

"They got it so wrong for such a long time that they don't ever want to re-visit their past. Anyway, It seems I've got nothing to do now but remind them, though I will make a point of being somewhat more civilised with them than they were with Tara's people and the others." He wasn't sure if her memories would include anyone other than her 'sister'.

"Wow." It seemed to be one of her favourite words, but she said it loud enough to turn the head of the young deckhand, yet again. Then she leaned towards him to look out his window for a better view. He turned just in time to see five black shapes leap from the water alongside the boat in a tight elongated formation. They were like penguins with white bellies and Jack, still hanging over the rails, shouted to the others when they popped up right under his nose. His shout sent them speeding away from the lifeboat into deeper water.

"I've never seen penguins in Ireland, have you?" She asked earnestly.

"No. Except for the zoo of course." He tried to wipe his window clean so she could get a better view but just then, the engine on the inflatable announced its final departure from Skellig. The screaming outboard cut through the gull chatter to make the 'penguins' nervous and they dived like it was something they'd choreographed, almost connected to each other, beak to tail.

"Then what are they?"

To him, they were gatecrashers from two previous existences. One was with Tara and the other more recent, when he'd seen the very sad sight of a stuffed one in London's Natural Museum.

"I'm almost positive they're great auks." His look told her he was serious.

"But haven't they been extinct since … well … way back?" Those big eyes practically beamed through him. "Well? Haven't they?"

The brash young doctor had apparently been left behind on Skellig and he realised that her haughty arrogance was more than likely an act. It was her way of discouraging people from getting too close for one reason or another. It shot down mutual attractions before they could get going, like a defence mechanism.

He was trained to see strengths and weaknesses and that presented him with an even younger version of her, who was most likely on the receiving end of bullying. Kids can be merciless and especially when they see 'gingers' or 'nerds' as just too different and she was very much both. He'd seen his own sister grow up and for a couple of years she did whatever it took to make herself invisible. Cora had likely become so supercritical that she couldn't differentiate between physical attraction and unwanted attention.

"Apparently not." He smiled broadly, but chose not to speculate on the role that Skellig might have played in the auk's apparently miraculous re-introduction.

The radio continued to squawk intermittently while the small derrick hoisted the inflatable into a slot on the cabin's roof. When the tone from the twin diesels was raised a notch to ease them out into the ocean, a connection like an umbilical, between himself and Skellig was pulled taut. When they synchronised in pitch and resonance, the throttles were eased up further and they arced around towards Dooah's Kingdom.

They had to speak louder to be heard, but the noise also ensured discretion.

"You told me why you felt obliged to keep your admirers at a distance but maybe that's something you should ease up on, now that you're twenty-two and the world is your oyster at last."

"It's that obvious?" Though she didn't seem too surprised that he'd seen through her, like it didn't matter anymore.

"Yes, and you don't need to be insecure either. You're actually nothing like the ugly duckling you used to think you were."

"Wow. You really do fancy yourself as a shrink and maybe as something else as well but like I said, I do have options, so no need to worry about me. That said, I'm happy you're coming around to the fact that Tara is still alive in her own way, but also very different from how you probably remember her."

They were coming abeam Little Skellig when the umbilical finally snapped. The fear he had of losing the security of Skellig, or of Tearmann, which was also his last connection to Tara evaporated. He knew he was going home a much wealthier man for the experience. He turned around to watch it through the open door and he kept his eyes there while it shrank. Then he realised that the part he was taking with him was growing. He wasn't leaving Skellig at all and she didn't miss the slow replay of the same Tara smile.

"You don't have to answer and I probably shouldn't ask, but how can two people be so blissfully in love, out there … during winter?" Having practically slandered him for it earlier, and having experienced some of it for herself through genetic memory, he wondered why she needed to hear him say anything.

She held the brooch in her right hand and turned it over slowly, from top to bottom, just as Tara had, and then swept her hair aside, also just as she would. Ignatius noticed then that where Cora was light, Tara was dark but they were beginning to look pretty much the same otherwise. They were identical opposites, each a photographic negative of the other, one flesh and bone and the other, memories.

"The best way I can describe it, would be like pouring yourself out into the same cup as someone else and then letting them stir it until they're happy, before filling yourself up again." He'd come up with that one during an Examen a few days before … well … in 478AD.

"You'd need to trust someone a whole lot to risk opening up like that … but you do express it nicely." She said and pushed herself back in her seat to maybe think about that or about something else. It was pretty much impossible to tell what might be going on inside that head. Having made the observation that they could have been anything but identical twins, he reached into one of those small zipped pockets designed to keep the most valuable possessions safe.

"This is no good to me now and it was supposed to be a birthday present for someone we know, so I want you to have it. It's only bronze, nothing like your brooch, but it's genuine bronze-age bronze and very much hand made with too much TLC to be considered really cool these days." He passed it over to her slowly, giving himself time to change his mind and surprising himself when he didn't.

"Wow. That's really it? You have no idea how important that is. I can only just about remember not taking it because it was the last thing before … well … something unpleasant." She pocketed the brooch but took her time to carefully zip the pocket closed before turning her full attention to the ring, like it was a very fragile thing and once again, turned it over top to bottom in the way he'd seen only one person do before.

"I'm sorry it doesn't have your name but it does have the actual date."

She read it out aloud. "'Tara' 'XX11' 'AD' 'CCCCLXXVIII', that's twenty-two right?"

"Yeah." Her latin wasn't great either it seemed, and he laughed but his eyes still welled up.

"And that long string of letters would read 478 in modern numbers." He threw in.

"That's a lot of letters for just a three digits." She laughed for him and then switched to the subject of her name.

"Tara, Cora, Gina, Hona, the list goes on. My 'parents' have never been very imaginative when it came to names for me slash us. It was always two syllables and no more, with the second one invariably an 'a'. So, it's near enough my name, but Tara and me are closer than you might think, so it makes no difference."

It was no good to him but it was amazing what it meant to her, and he got no small pleasure from the very simple pleasure of watching her own just a little bit more of herself. They sat quietly as Skellig fell even further behind. Another look aft and the part with the waves washing the rocks had slid out of view, giving the impression it was beginning to sink into the sea, an Atlantis of sorts.

"The Jesuits will probably kick you out or worse when they learn about your upcoming self-assignment."

"Probably." He was able to laugh this time and he caught the young deckhand sneaking a look at her. It struck him then that Cora was probably only a little older than the shy young man and that made them easily the youngest people on board.

"By the way … how did you get yourself on the panel for this kind of work? I would have thought that you'd need some actual experience and maybe a nomination or two?"

"That was the weirdest thing." She leaned forward, glancing to her left just in time to see a red faced young man turn rapidly away, but the innocence of it escaped her.

"I planned to come out here one day, to look for the brooch, but you just can't underestimate the zest for life that you get when you don't wake up dead on your twenty-second birthday."

That was absolutely hysterical and he struggled to stifle his reaction, but she didn't hold back. "I just took off this morning … I mean, I just had to … but I didn't know there were no tours in winter. Portmagee is like a morgue off-season, so I went to the police station to ask for a name, to maybe hire a boat."

He had to interrupt because his eyes were welling up again, but for a different set of reasons. "Didn't you know how much that was going to cost?" But he didn't give her a chance to answer. "And assuming you do carry wads of cash, you were really lucky with this weather. It's because of the weather that they close it for winter. Take it from me, I know."

She didn't care. She was a storyteller with a story to tell and he was only delaying her. telling of it. "Yeah, yeah. Anyway, I hear the sergeant … McSweeney. He's a real sweetheart by the way, and he's raving about a Jesuit Priest they just found alive on Skellig. Seems he was convinced that you didn't fall into the sea all by yourself." She sat up straight to let him ingest that.

"Why would he think that?" Asked Ignatius but then waved his own question away. "But you don't just walk onto a lifeboat. Do you?"

She came forward again but much closer this time and he found himself enjoying the proximity. "No. I had to tell a white lie about being the best trauma doctor in Munster and I suggested that he was so lucky that I just happened to drop by."

"And he bought that?"

"Why not … he even offered to get me their emergency medical bag. You don't think a doctor like me carries all that gear around with them … just in case … do you? Anyway, speaking of money, I've just started my medical practise and so I've only got a small apartment, but it's got two rooms and you're welcome to one of them … until you get organised …"

Ignatius was bewildered by the way she could change subjects mid-breath, but also by how big her heart was under all the pretence. "You don't owe me anything and anyway, I'll be fine. I'm a big boy now."

"But I feel like I do. You deserve better than to face such a one sided fight with none of your friends around to help you." Now her eyes were showing a suggestion of more liquid content than normal.

None of us is ever alone. We either look like a sibling, a parent or a grandparent. Sometimes these genetic similarities skip generations before inexplicably manifesting themselves again and just then, there were aspects of Tara that just eased through Cora's less brittle armour to make themselves known. Colours and shades aside, Cora was more Tara where it mattered. Much more than he would have thought possible on the way down Skellig.

"Well, if that's the case, then it was never your debt to repay and anyway, I'm lucky enough to have the family home intact and I should easily get a teaching job, so I'll be able to afford my undertakings until I can attract some sponsors. Then there's going to be so much flak and as you said, you have other options that you had to neglect, and you'll really need some space to explore them now. You definitely don't need me in your way."

"Yeah. But you've no money for groceries or for a hospital stay and they won't pay anything for you, so maybe you should take it for a while at least, so I can keep you under observation for a few days and anyway … I think you might have just bumped yourself onto my option list."

EPILOGUE

“That’s going to be more difficult than you realise.” There was definitely chemistry and it was very romantically spontaneous, but Ignatius was a realist. The fact was, that with her previously impenetrable facade in tatters, she appeared to be every bit as naive as she accused Tara of being. It occurred to him then that in its simplest form, maybe evolution was just a gift of more masks to hide behind. However, as small sparks continued to jump between them like static, even saying goodbye to her was beginning to look like it might be an ordeal. It was all just far too much and way too soon.

“You’re right. It’s going to be nearly impossible.” She agreed, though sadly it seemed, but that was music to his ears and he tried not to smile.

“I should have told you I’m an only child and a bit of a Daddy’s girl.”

“What’s that got to do with anything?” His senses told him that she had to be joking, but her straight face told him otherwise.

“Well. I love him loads and I see a lot of him and that can’t change.”

“Nor should it.” To anyone else, she would be just mildly upset but to him, she was becoming more and more possessed by her long lost sister.

“But he despises priests.” She said, giggling.

“Then we have that in common.” He agreed and then realised that she’d swung the discussion slash argument around. He was supposed to be arguing his way out.

“But even more than priests, he’s always lecturing me about the dangers of dating older men.” She was straight faced again.

“But never mind … my mother is a fervent Catholic.”

“Are you being serious?” Ignatius didn’t know whether to laugh or cry.

“Yeah. They’re a bit weird, but that would probably explain me.”

He looked at her in disbelief. There was just no saying no.

No rescue finishes when you step off a lifeboat, down from a helicopter or you finally come to on the beach, with anxious and also merely curious faces filling your patch of sky.

Standard operating procedure requires you to be taken to a hospital, where the paramedic(s) will ‘hand’ you over to medical personnel for their further evaluation and then the tests begin. Also, a qualified doctor taking early possession of you while the rescue is still in progress doesn't necessarily mean that you get a shortcut. In the case of Reverend Father Ignatius Moloney's rescue from Skellig, it meant paperwork and lot's of it but all things end, and then it was dark.

"OK, but seriously … just until I get on my feet."

It was like she never heard him.

"You really do need a bath y'know," She said and followed with, "- and a shave and I know a good dentist … and that's my car over there."

"It's a Porsche!" It came out as more shout than simple observation.

"Yeah. I do love cars and anyway, up until this morning it didn't look like I'd have to pay it off."

Cora Quinn casually clicked her key and then jumped inside. His mouth was still open when she reached over to push the passenger door open for him. He breathed in his affirmation that nothing smells quite as good as new car leather, until she turned the key and the engine purred into life. He looked over to note that she was nothing short of a revelation … and then he remembered.

"You do know that we'll have to come back very soon." He said.

"Why? We've both got a lot more than we bargained for and Dad says you should always quit when ahead."

“Your Dad sounds like a wise man Cora, but I’m going to need something very convincing for the Jesuits and though I never imagined formally presenting it, it’s probably everything that I’ll need.”

“What’s that?” She asked.

“Somewhere on Skellig there’s what is effectively a full thesis in old vellum, written in a style unique to the period and to the essence of what it is to be spiritual. It’s probably the earliest example of Hisperica Famina in existence. We called it Revelatio Pluvit, which means ‘Revelation Rains’. The thing is, it could have been written with my mission in mind … in fact … maybe it was … and I think I know where they left it.” He was ecstatic.

“Wow. What does it say?”

“Well. I’m going to have to explain spirituality to people who have convinced themselves that it’s all about religion, which it isn’t. In an ideal world I could do that by bringing each of them to Skellig to show them that prayer books are redundant, but that’s impossible. With ‘Revelation Rains’, I can bring Skellig to them, and to everyone else who can’t make it out there.”

“Wow. What does it say?” She asked again, in the very same tones.

“It says simply everything.”

When her expression didn't change, he corrected himself.

"What I mean is, it says everything, but very simply."

Other Books

by Denis McClean

The four books of the 'Thin Places' Series of Novellas

are

'Fanore', 'Erris', 'Blasket' and 'Skellig',

Denis also wrote:-

Catalysis - Book 1 of The Catalysis Trilogy (Changes Imposed)

Ochre - Book 2 of The Catalysis Trilogy (Destiny Takes You …)

Imago - Catalysis Trilogy Finale (Are Some Destinies immune from Destiny?)

The Catalysis Trilogy is also available in one cover - Complete

Book of Plebs - Revelations Still Rains!

More About

http://denismcclean.blogspot.ie/

Printed in Great Britain
by Amazon

44601132R00136